**'B**████████████████**y,
tears o**████████████████**ng her
eyes.**

█ hated Zahir, and hated herself more, yet
█en now, when he was looking down his arro-
█nt nose at her, she longed to trace her fingers
█ver the hard planes of his face and feel the
█ush of his lips on hers in a kiss of tenderness
█ther than blazing passion.

█om the first moment she had seen him she
█d felt a connection with him that she did not
█derstand. It couldn't be love, she told herself.
█ wasn't possible to love and hate someone
█multaneously—was it? And if it was love,
█en she was an even bigger fool than she had
█lieved, because Zahir was as harsh and unfor-
█ving as the desert. His heart was hewn from
█anite, and he would never love her.

**Chantelle Shaw** lives on the Kent coast, five minutes from the sea, and does much of her thinking about the characters in her books while walking on the beach. She's been an avid reader from an early age. Her schoolfriends used to hide their books when she visited—but Chantelle would retreat into her own world, and still writes stories in her head all the time. Chantelle has been blissfully married to her own tall, dark and very patient hero for over twenty years, and has six children. She began to read Mills & Boon® as a teenager, and throughout the years of being a stay-at-home mum to her brood found romantic fiction helped her to stay sane! She enjoys reading and writing about strong-willed, feisty women, and even stronger willed sexy heroes. Chantelle is at her happiest when writing. She is particularly inspired while cooking dinner, which unfortunately results in a lot of culinary disasters! She also loves gardening, walking, and eating chocolate (followed by more walking!).

# AT THE SHEIKH'S BIDDING

BY
CHANTELLE SHAW

## MILLS & BOON™
*Pure reading pleasure*™

All the characters in this book have no existence outside the imagination of the author, and have no relation whatsoever to anyone bearing the same name or names. They are not even distantly inspired by any individual known or unknown to the author, and all the incidents are pure invention.

First published in Great Britain 2008
Harlequin Mills & Boon Limited,
Eton House, 18-24 Paradise Road, Richmond, Surrey TW9 1SR

© Chantelle Shaw 2008

ISBN: 978 0 263 86467 0

Set in Times Roman 10½ on 13 pt
01-1008-48502

Printed and bound in Spain
by Litografia Rosés, S.A., Barcelona

# AT THE SHEIKH'S BIDDING

# CHAPTER ONE

*The Royal Palace in the desert kingdom of Qubbah.*

PRINCE ZAHIR BIN KAHLID AL MUNTASSIR swept through the palace towards King Kahlid's private quarters, the expression on his handsome face so grimly forbidding that the guards quickly jumped aside to allow him to pass. 'How is he?' he demanded, when his father's servant A'waan greeted him with a bow.

'Sleeping, sire—the doctor gave him a sedative and instructed that His Highness should be allowed to rest,' A'waan murmured, hovering anxiously in front of the door leading to the King's bedroom.

'It's all right, A'waan, I have no intention of disturbing him,' Zahir assured the servant. 'The news of Prince Faisal's death has been a great shock to all of us, but especially to my father.'

'His Highness is deeply saddened. He is not properly recovered from the virus he contracted recently, and I fear that the news will prove too much for him,' A'waan said gravely. 'Your father's one glimmer of joy is the discovery that he has a grandson—a child who is now an orphan.'

Zahir's jaw clenched as he fought to control his emotions while A'waan continued.

'It is His Highness's dearest wish that you should travel to England and bring the child back to Qubbah.'

'I am well aware of my father's wishes,' Zahir said tightly. He crossed to the window and stared out over the stunning formal gardens and the ornate fountains that splashed into an azure pool. Within the grounds of the palace the desert had been tamed, but beyond the walls of the twelfth-century fortress it stretched outward in an endless sea of scorching golden sands.

The setting sun was suspended like a huge golden orb, the sky around it streaked with shades of pink and red. He remembered the times he and Faisal had raced their horses across the sands, or released their falcons and watched them soar across the dense blue sky. More than brothers, they had been the best of friends, but the bond between them had been broken—and all because they had both fallen in love with the same woman. Zahir's brows drew together in a slashing frown. *Love*, he had discovered, *was a destructive emotion and he would never allow it to rule his heart or mind again.*

A'waan spoke again. 'As you know, your father always hoped to be reconciled with his eldest son, and that, on his death the Prince would return to Qubbah to rule. But now Prince Faisal is dead, and there is unrest in the kingdom while the people wait for the King to announce his successor. Forgive me for my presumption…' the elderly servant shifted nervously beneath Zahir's narrow-eyed stare '…but I know His Highness longs for you to appoint a deputy to head your business interests in America, so that you can settle permanently in Qubbah—and take a wife. Now, more than ever, it is your duty, sire.'

Zahir threw back his head proudly and glared at the servant.

'I do not need lessons from you on my duty,' he snapped coldly. 'You forget your place, A'waan.' He understood only too well that his brother's death meant that from now on his life would no longer be his own. He would not shirk his responsibility to the kingdom his family had ruled for generations—but marriage was a different matter. 'If you remember, I was about to be married six years ago, to a woman of my father's choosing—and what a debacle that turned out to be. I will marry when I am good and ready.' He swung abruptly away from the window and strode across the room, pausing briefly to glance back at the servant. 'When my father wakes, tell him I have gone to England.'

*Ingledean House—North Yorkshire Moors*

'Erin! There's a Gordon Straker here to see you,' announced Alice Trent, cook and housekeeper at Ingledean House, when Erin walked into the kitchen. 'He says he's Faisal's solicitor, and he mentioned something about the will.'

'Oh, yes.' Erin nodded. 'I spoke to him on the phone a couple of days ago and he said he would be travelling up from London.'

'Well, he's waiting in the library.' Alice paused in her task of peeling potatoes and stared at Erin's dishevelled appearance. 'What on earth have you been doing? You look as though you've been down a coal mine.'

'Clearing out the big spare bedroom.' Erin glanced ruefully at the streaks of dust on her jeans. 'Kazim's nursery is too small to store all his toys now that he's sleeping in a proper bed. The spare room will make a perfect playroom. I need to keep busy,' she added defensively, when Alice's brows lifted.

It was fine when Kazim was awake, keeping a lively three-year-old entertained took up all her time, but she had come to dread his afternoon nap—an hour of peace and solitude that gave her time to think.

It was almost three weeks since Faisal's funeral. His death had been expected—he had told her a year ago that the tumour on his brain was inoperable—and she was glad that he was now at peace, perhaps reunited with his beloved Maryam. But he had been her friend; she missed him, and she could not stem the feeling of panic that regularly swept through her whenever she thought about the future. Kazim's well-being was totally her responsibility now, and she was terrified that she would somehow let him down.

She turned to watch the toddler, who had preceded her into the kitchen and was now busy pulling open the cupboards and investigating their contents. Kazim was singing 'The Wheels on the Bus', and Erin's heart clenched at the sound of his innocent, high-pitched voice. He'd asked for Faisal a few times, but had seemed to understand when she'd gently explained that Daddy had fallen asleep for ever.

It had been the hardest thing she had ever had to do in her life, and the memory of Kazim's grave little face as he had sat on her knee still brought tears to her eyes. But, although he had been a little more clingy than usual, he seemed to have accepted the news remarkably well—perhaps because he was too young to comprehend that he was now totally alone in the world.

But he is not alone, Erin thought fiercely. True, he had no living relatives, but he had her, and she would love him and protect him for as long as he needed her—just as she had promised his father.

'I've made some tea.' Alice's voice broke into her thoughts. 'If you want to take it up, I'll keep an eye on Kazim.'

Erin glanced at the tray. 'Why have you set out three cups, Alice?'

'Mr Straker has brought someone with him. Gave me quite a turn, actually, when he walked through the front door—for a moment I thought he was Faisal's ghost.' The cook gave a self-conscious laugh. 'I expect it was just a trick of the light. He's obviously from the Middle East—rather gorgeous; you know, tall, dark and indecently handsome. And his features did remind me of the master,' she added slowly. 'Do you think he could be a relative?'

An inexplicable feeling of unease settled in the pit of Erin's stomach. 'Faisal had no family,' she explained quickly. 'I don't know who this man is, but he's probably one of Faisal's business associates. I'd better go up and meet them,' she said, picking up the tray.

Alice cast a disparaging look at her old clothes. 'I would suggest you go and change first, but there's no time. It's snowing again, and I know Mr Straker is anxious to get back to town before the weather closes in.'

Erin hurried out of the kitchen, and as she crossed the oak-panelled hall she caught sight of her reflection in the mirror and grimaced. Her faded jeans and tee shirt were grubbier than she'd realised, and her hair, which she had secured in a long plait, had worked loose, so that riotous stray curls were framing her face. But it was unlikely that Gordon Straker or his companion would have any interest in her appearance, she told herself as she balanced the tray on one hand and opened the library door—coming to such an abrupt halt that the delicate bone china cups rattled precariously on their saucers.

A man was standing by the window, staring out over the bleak view of the moors. For a few seconds her heart seemed to stop beating, and she understood what Alice had meant when she'd said she had thought she seen Faisal's ghost. The stranger's profile was achingly familiar, as was his silky black hair and olive-gold skin. But then he turned his head—and common sense replaced her wild flight of imagination.

This man was no spectre, he was very much alive. And his resemblance to Faisal was simply due to his dark colouring and exotic looks, she told herself impatiently. He was wearing a superbly tailored dark grey suit that accentuated his lean, hard body, and Erin was immediately struck by his height, estimating that he must be five or six inches over six feet tall. Impressive broad shoulders indicated an awesome degree of strength and power, but it was his face that trapped her gaze and caused her heart to thud painfully beneath her ribcage.

His hair was cropped uncompromisingly short, and his eyes were as dark as midnight beneath heavy black brows. His nose was slightly hooked, but that did not detract from the perfection of his sculpted face with its sharply delineated cheekbones and square, determined jaw. He was the epitome of masculine beauty, she thought helplessly, her breath catching in her throat. He was so gorgeous he was almost unreal, as if he had been airbrushed to perfection—but he wasn't an image from a magazine. He was a flesh-and-blood man, and she was startled by the effect he had on her.

The man subjected her to a long, cool stare and Erin felt herself blush. 'Hello, I've brought some tea. You're probably freezing. The central heating system here at Ingledean is antiquated.'

Black eyebrows winged upwards and her cheeks burned hotter. The man's resemblance to Faisal could not be denied— but her feelings for Faisal had been based on friendship and affection. Neither he nor any other man had ever evoked this shocking, wildfire sexual desire that was coursing through her veins. She felt unnerved by the stranger's raw masculinity, and she realised that she was gaping at him. Forcing herself to breathe normally, she walked across to the desk and set down the tray.

'I'm Erin.' She smiled hesitantly, half extended her hand and waited for him to return the introduction, her smile fading when he made no reply.

'You may pour the tea and then go. Your presence will no longer be necessary,' he informed her dismissively, in a clipped, haughty tone, before he swung round and resumed his contemplation of the snow that was now swirling outside the window.

Erin stared at the rigid line of his back, shocked into silence by his arrogance. Just who did he think he was? And how dared he speak to her in that high and mighty manner, as if she was some lowly scullery maid from a Victorian melodrama?

Shock gave way to anger. She'd spent most of her formative years feeling worthless—until her foster parents had rescued her from a life that had been rapidly going into freefall and insisted that she was a valued member of society, rather than a nobody from the gutter. But the fragile self-confidence she'd gained while living with John and Anne Black was easily dented, and inside she was still the unloved child and rebellious teenager who had been dumped in a care home after her mother's final and fatal heroin fix.

She bit her lip and picked up the teapot, torn between the urge to slink from the room and the temptation to tell the stranger exactly what he could do with the damn tea. But before she could speak the library door swung open, and the spare, grey-haired solicitor she had met once when she had visited London with Faisal hurried into the room.

'Ah, Erin, tea—wonderful.' Gordon Straker greeted her enthusiastically. His brief smile encompassed both Erin and the man at the window, but the sight of the thickly falling snow caused him to frown, and he glanced at his watch as he sat down and picked up the sheaf of documents on the desk in front of him. 'Take a seat, both of you, and we'll begin, shall we?' he said briskly, oblivious to the stranger's harsh frown. 'I won't keep you long. Faisal's last will and testament is very straightforward.'

Zahir remained standing, his eyes narrowing as he watched the maid pull out a chair. He was again aware of the same hollow feeling in his stomach and the uncomfortable tightening sensation in his chest—as if he had been winded—that had gripped him when she had first entered the room.

She was quite possibly the most beautiful woman he had ever seen, he acknowledged, irritated by his body's involuntary reaction to her as sexual awareness flooded through his veins. The perfect symmetry of her face was riveting, and he stared at her, drinking in every detail of her high cheekbones, the wide, clear grey eyes that surveyed him from beneath finely arched hazel brows, her small, straight nose and the mouth that was a fraction too wide, the lips soft and full and infinitely kissable.

A thick braid of auburn hair fell down her back, almost to her waist, the colour reminding him of the rich red hues of leaves in the fall. Years ago, when he had been a student at Harvard, he had been entranced by the stunning palette of colours that Mother Nature used to herald autumn in New England. Now he felt an overwhelming urge to untie the ribbon that secured the woman's hair and run his fingers through the mass of rippling red-gold silk.

His eyes slid lower, skimmed the small, firm breasts outlined beneath her tee shirt, and then moved down to her slender waist, narrow hips and long legs, encased in faded denim. Even at the end of his life Faisal had clearly not lost his discerning eye for gorgeous women if his domestic staff were anything to go by, Zahir thought sardonically. Although he would have expected the household staff to wear some sort of uniform rather than a pair of sexy, tight jeans.

But why had the solicitor asked this woman—whom he assumed from her appearance to be a member of the household staff—to stay while he discussed Faisal's private affairs? Could she be a beneficiary in Faisal's will? She was very lovely, and Faisal had been alone… But the idea that his brother had bequeathed her some token payment for favours rendered was curiously unpalatable, and he silently cursed his overactive imagination.

His gaze locked with hers, and for a second something flared between them, some indefinable chemistry that clearly shocked her as it shocked him. But almost instantly the flash of awareness in her eyes dulled and was replaced with confusion. The silence in the room was broken by the solicitor's discreet cough. The sound reminded Zahir that he was not here to eye up members of the domestic staff. Smothering a curse, he strode over to the desk, seized a chair and sat down, at the same time as the maid subsided into the seat next to him.

Gordon Straker cleared his throat and began to read. 'I, Faisal bin Kahlid al Muntassir leave my entire estate, including Ingledean House and all its contents, to my wife.'

From the corner of her eye Erin saw the unknown man jerk

even more upright in his chair, and his voice was sharp with impatience when he spoke. 'I understand that my sister-in-law died three years ago. This will is invalid. There must be another updated one,' he snapped haughtily.

Gordon Straker glanced at him steadily over the wire rims of his spectacles and said, in a wintry tone, 'I assure you that this is the most recent will. My client asked me to draw it up ten months ago.' The solicitor hesitated, his gaze moving between the two shocked faces staring at him across the desk. Comprehension slowly dawned, and he shook his head.

'Forgive me. I did not introduce you because I assumed that the two of you already knew each other…that you had met… at the wedding.' His confusion and embarrassment deepened. 'But clearly not,' he added slowly, when they continued to stare blankly back at him. 'My apologies…it never occurred to me that you were unaware of each other's identity… Erin, may I introduce Sheikh Zahir bin Kahlid al Muntassir— Faisal's brother. Sheikh Zahir, this is Erin—Faisal's second wife.'

The book-lined walls of the library seemed to tilt alarmingly, and Erin gripped the edge of the desk as she struggled to comprehend Gordon Straker's words. 'But Faisal told me he had no family,' she mumbled, her gaze swinging frantically from the solicitor's genial face to the man beside her, whose expression was so coldly arrogant that ice slithered down her spine.

'There must be some mistake.' Zahir addressed the man seated opposite him, his clipped tones shattering the tense silence. Shock ricocheted through him, and with it a fierce and inexplicable bolt of fury that overrode the grief that had consumed him since he had learned of Faisal's death.

What bitter irony that once again he had lost out to his brother—just as he had done six years ago, he brooded grimly. This woman, with her slumbrous, woodsmoke-coloured eyes and sensual, pouting mouth, had been Faisal's *wife*. Faisal must have released her glorious hair and watched it tumble down her back. He would have stroked his hands over her milky-pale naked flesh…just as he, Zahir, had fantasised about doing from the moment he had laid eyes on her.

*And even the knowledge that she had been his brother's widow for little more than two weeks did not lessen his awareness of her, or diminish the primitive urge he felt to crush her mouth beneath his and then strip the clothes from her body and spread her across the desk, ready for his possession.*

His lip curled in self-disgust, and he could not bring himself to look at her while he exerted iron will-power over his rampaging hormones. What did it matter who she was or what her relationship had been with Faisal? he asked himself impatiently. His wealth, combined with the good-looks that he acknowledged were a fortunate accident of birth, meant that he could take his pick from a limitless supply of beautiful women—and he did so, frequently. He did not need his brother's leftovers. There was only one reason why he was here, only one thing he was interested in.

He stood up and walked back over to the window, needing to put some distance between himself and the woman who was having such a disturbing effect on him.

Erin jumped to her feet and glared at him. 'It's no mistake, I assure you,' she said hotly. 'I was Faisal's wife, and I have a marriage certificate to prove it.'

Zahir's brows lifted. 'My apologies—I had no idea. Your

attire hardly befits your position as the wife of a sheikh. I assumed you were a menial domestic.'

Hot colour flooded Erin's face as she felt his eyes trail over her in a scathing assessment of her appearance, and she silently cursed the fact that she hadn't taken the trouble to change into more presentable clothes for her meeting with Gordon Straker. But, to be fair, she had not expected to be confronted by an arrogant, devilishly sexy sheikh who, astoundingly, happened to be Faisal's brother.

Her temper, which had been simmering ever since he had spoken to her so dismissively when she had brought in the tea tray, flared into life. She recalled how he had looked at her when she had first walked into the library, the way his eyes had slid boldly over her as if he were mentally undressing her. Presumably he thought it acceptable to take a servant to bed, but not for her to marry his brother, she thought furiously.

She lifted her chin and met Zahir bin Kahlid al Muntassir's gaze, her grey eyes stormy and belligerent. But the undisguised sexual heat in his dark depths sent an answering quiver of awareness down her spine, and it was only when he finally broke eye contact that she realised she had been holding her breath.

'My brother was estranged from his family for the past six years,' he explained coolly.

Erin's insides churned at the word 'family'. What *family*? Faisal had insisted that he had no relatives, and yet not only did it seem that he had a brother, but from the sound of it other family members also existed. Why had he lied to her? And if Faisal had been estranged from his family how had his brother known about his death? Her unease intensified, and solidified into fear when Zahir spoke again.

'I was unaware, until I received the letter Faisal instructed

Mr Straker to send after his death, that my sister-in-law died three years ago. Faisal made no mention in that letter that he had remarried,' he added pointedly, his eyes flicking briefly over Erin. 'I was also unaware until two weeks ago that my brother had a son—a child who is now an orphan.'

He flicked his gaze to Erin once more, his eyes as black and hard as polished jet. 'As Faisal's sole beneficiary, you are now a very wealthy woman,' he drawled. 'But I am not interested in the money, and you are certainly welcome to this draughty monstrosity of a house,' he added disparagingly, casting a brief glance around the library, where the fire burning in the grate did little to raise the temperature of the room.

'My only interest is in my nephew, Kazim. I assume he has been well cared for since Faisal's death?' He overrode Erin's attempt to speak and announced coolly, 'I have come to take him to his father's homeland, Qubbah, so that he may be brought up by his family. Please inform his nanny, or whoever is in charge of him, that I wish to meet him, and ask them to pack his personal possessions as quickly as possible. I want to leave before the weather gets any worse.'

Erin gaped at him, her heart thumping erratically in her chest. 'You're not taking Kazim anywhere,' she snapped, disbelief and outrage at his high-handedness causing a red mist of anger to swirl in front of her eyes. 'When I married Faisal, I adopted Kazim as my own child. I am his legal parent, and he is staying right here at Ingledean. *This* is his home,' she finished fiercely, refusing to feel intimidated by Zahir's furious expression.

Black brows lowered in a slashing frown. 'Is this true?'

Once again he'd addressed the solicitor, but Erin was fed up with being treated as if she was part of the furniture, and she glared at him, her hands on her hips and her eyes blazing.

'Damn right, it's true. Kazim is legally my son, and I won't allow you to take him. You have no rights to him.'

'We'll see about that—or rather my lawyers will,' Zahir snapped icily.

His jaw tightened. In all his thirty-six years he had never been spoken to in such a disrespectful manner—and certainly not by a woman. Under his father's rule Qubbah had gradually become a more liberal kingdom, and he himself had spent much of his life in the US and Europe, where he accepted that men and women were equals, but he was a prince and he was used to being treated accordingly—to being fawned on, he admitted honestly, and to the unashamed adoration of women from both cultures.

He was *not* used to being yelled at by a flame-haired banshee, and the fact that Erin looked even more gorgeous when she was angry was no help at all. She was breathing hard, and he found himself fixated by the frantic rise and fall of her small breasts. Irritation, and another far more primitive emotion surged through him. He could not remember ever wanting a woman with such shaming urgency, but this woman was definitely out of bounds—Faisal's widow and, apparently, the adoptive mother of his son.

Zahir spun round and raked a hand through his hair. Hell, she was an unforeseen complication he could do without, he thought furiously. On the other side of the world an old and heartbroken man was waiting to greet his grandson. He had promised his father he would bring Faisal's son to Qubbah, and he would not fail him. But clearly the situation was not as straightforward as he had assumed. He knew without conceit that he was a brilliant businessman and a shrewd tactician, feared and revered in the boardroom, but for the first time in his life he was at a loss to know what to do next, and he hated the feeling.

'I can't believe you thought you could just turn up here and whisk a three-year-old child off to another country, when he doesn't even know you,' Erin threw at him. 'Kazim is little more than a baby, for heaven's sake, who has just lost his father. Didn't it occur to you that he would be terrified at being dragged off by a complete stranger?'

'I was not going to *drag* him anywhere,' Zahir snapped, stung by her criticism. 'I came here alone today, rather than with my usual team of staff, so that he would have a chance to get to know me. My brother must have known I would come for him once I learned of his existence,' he added harshly. 'I assumed Kazim's nanny had been instructed to continue caring for him until I arrived. I have already employed a highly qualified and experienced nanny to take charge of him in Qubbah.'

Fear gripped Erin, and her confusion intensified, but she hid both emotions. 'Well, I'm sorry you've had a wasted journey,' she said, forcing herself to sound calm. 'But Faisal made it clear that he wanted Kazim to grow up in England—with me. He asked me to adopt Kazim, and I was happy to do so.'

'In that case, why did he make no mention of you in his letter?'

Zahir had voiced the question that Erin could not answer, but she was saved from having to try when Gordon Straker stood up.

'I'm sorry to interrupt, but it looks as though the weather is getting worse, and I have a train to catch,' he said apologetically. He was already pulling on his coat, glancing worriedly out of the window at the heavy sky that warned snow was likely to continue falling for many hours yet. 'Erin, if you need my advice at all…' He hesitated and turned his eyes briefly to Zahir before moving them back to Erin. 'Please contact me at my London office, any time.' He walked towards the door, but paused when Zahir spoke sharply.

'Are you sure there is nothing in the will about the child? No clause stipulating who should care for Kazim—no financial provision made for him?'

'No,' the solicitor replied simply. 'Your brother left everything to Erin—in the expectation, I imagine, that she would provide for Kazim.'

'Which I will,' Erin burst out fiercely, infuriated at Zahir's plainly sceptical expression. 'I love Kazim as if he was my own child.'

'Really?' Zahir swung away from her and gave a harsh laugh. Erin sounded convincing, but he found it impossible to believe that she was prepared to devote her life to a child who was not her own flesh and blood out of love. Not when his own mother had abandoned him.

He had barely given his mother a thought for the past decade, Zahir realised with a jolt. Georgina had been his father's second wife, an American who, according to his three older half-sisters, had found it difficult to settle to the life of strict protocol demanded of wife to the King of Qubbah. Zahir had not known that, and as a young boy he had simply accepted her frequent trips back to the US and waited impatiently for her to return to the palace. But when he was eleven she had not returned, and he'd never seen her or spoken to her again.

His father had explained that she was busy looking after her sick mother and couldn't come back. Zahir had missed her desperately, and for a long time after she had gone he had kept her silk robe hidden beneath his pillow and wept into it every night. But when he was fourteen he learned the truth—that she had refused to live in Qubbah any longer and had accepted a huge financial settlement from his father in return for not seeking custody of her only son.

She had sold him—and he had never cried again after he'd found out, nor spared her another thought. But he had learned a valuable lesson about love and trust, Zahir conceded bitterly—a lesson that had been reinforced six years ago, when he had been betrayed by the only other woman he had ever loved.

Noises from beyond the library door catapulted him back to the present: the sound of a child crying mingled with a distinctive, broad Yorkshire accent. A moment later the door was flung open and a woman appeared with a hysterical toddler her arms.

'Sorry to disturb you.' She addressed Erin, oblivious to the tension in the room. 'But Kazim has banged his head on the kitchen table. You know how he runs everywhere. Look, there's a lump the size of an egg come up on his forehead, but he won't let me console him—he wants you.'

Quickly Erin held out her arms and took the sobbing child from the cook, her heart clenching when he wrapped his arms around her neck and burrowed close. 'Shh, it's all right, darling. Let me look at your head.' She brushed his dark curls off his brow and inspected the livid bruise, before applying the ice pack Alice had handed her. 'That's quite a bump you've got there, but there's no real harm done.'

Kazim's sobs gradually subsided as she cuddled him. He smelled deliciously of soap and baby powder, and the intensity of her love for him squeezed her heart like a giant fist. She had adored him since he was three months old, and nothing would ever make her give him up, she vowed fiercely. But when she glanced up and saw Faisal's brother watching her, with his dark, forbidding gaze, she was filled with a sense of foreboding.

Alice heaved a sigh of relief. 'Kazim's a little daredevil,' she cheerfully informed the two men. 'He's always running and climbing, and he's constantly getting into mischief. Erin has her work cut out, looking after him.'

Erin saw Zahir frown and groaned silently. *Thanks, Alice— that's a real help.*

'Shouldn't you seek medical advice for his head injury?' he queried coldly.

Kazim was squirming in her arms, wanting to get down and clearly none the worse for his accident. 'He's fine,' Erin said tersely. 'He's a lively three year-old, for goodness' sake, I can't keep him wrapped in cotton wool. I'm a fully trained nanny and qualified in first-aid,' she continued, when Zahir looked unconvinced. 'I'm perfectly capable of looking after him.'

She lifted her chin and her eyes clashed with his cold, faintly contemptuous gaze. She hated his arrogance, but she could not look away from him. As she watched heat flared in those dark depths, and for a split second raw, sexual hunger gleamed beneath his heavy brows before his thick lashes fell, concealing his thoughts.

Shaken, she glanced at Gordon Straker, who was edging towards the door. 'Erin, I'm sorry, but I really must…'

'Yes, of course.' Making a swift decision, she set Kazim down and turned to Alice. 'Will you keep an eye on him while I see Mr Straker out?'

She hurried across the hall after the solicitor, and stopped him as he was about to open the front door. 'Mr Straker, when did Faisal give you the letter he instructed you to send to his brother after his death? Was it when he married me?' she queried huskily.

'Oh, no, it was about a month before he died. Until then I hadn't known Faisal had any family, and I see that the revelation has come as a shock to you too,' he added gently.

Erin bit her lip, feeling a sudden urge to confide in the kindly solicitor. 'From the moment Faisal learned that he was dying he was desperate to secure Kazim's future,' she explained urgently. 'I've cared for him since he was three months old. Faisal's wife died as a result of complications while giving birth, and when Faisal's illness was diagnosed a year ago he asked me to marry him to make it easier for me to adopt Kazim. He told me he had no other family and he didn't want Kazim to grow up in care—like I had.'

She hated talking about her past, and dropped her gaze from Gordon Straker's face as she continued in a low voice, 'My mother was a drug addict, who died when I was ten, and I spent the rest of my childhood in the care of Social Services. I was a troubled teenager, and I don't know where I would be now if I hadn't been fostered—maybe working the streets to pay for my next fix like my mother,' she confessed thickly. 'My foster father worked here at Ingledean, as a gardener, and when Faisal came here with his baby son he employed me as Kazim's nanny. Despite my background he knew I would love and protect Kazim as if he was my own child.'

She was hurt that Faisal had not been honest with her. He *did* have a family, and just before he'd died he had made the decision to tell them he had a son. Had he done so because he had begun to doubt her abilities to be a good mother to

Kazim? Had he decided that he wanted his estranged family to be involved in the little boy's upbringing after all?

All her old doubts and insecurities rose up inside her, but Gordon Straker opened the front door and a blast of icy wind whipped into the hall, snapping Erin out of her reverie.

The solicitor gave her a sympathetic smile. '*You* are Kazim's adoptive mother, Erin,' he said gently, 'and no one can take him from you. Only you can decide if it would be in his best interests to have some contact with his family in Qubbah.'

He turned up the collar of his coat and stepped into the snow, but paused to glance back at her. 'I've done a little investigating, and from what I've heard Sheikh Zahir bin Kahlid al Muntassir is an astute businessman and a risk-taker, respected on the world markets for his brilliance and daring. He is a man who is used to having his own way, and who pursues his goals with a ruthless determination, yet at the same time many people find him incredibly charming and persuasive—particularly women.' He gave a faint smile at her sudden heightened colour. 'All I'm saying is—tread carefully, Erin,' Gordon Straker warned softly, 'and don't let him bully you, my dear.'

'Don't worry, I won't,' Erin replied fiercely.

But as she flew back across the hall to the library, where she had left the Sheikh with her son, a shiver of trepidation ran through her. The moment she had seen Zahir she had been mesmerised by his spectacular looks and powerful sexual magnetism. The man spelt danger, and the predatory gleam she'd glimpsed in his dark eyes warned her to be on her guard.

# CHAPTER TWO

ZAHIR turned away from the window and the uninspiring view of snow-covered moors and found Kazim staring up at him, his chocolate-brown eyes wide with curiosity. Slowly he knelt down, so that he was on level with the toddler's gaze, and pain tugged in his chest. The little boy bore a marked resemblance to both his parents, and the sight of his small, lively face and impish grin made the tragedy of Faisal and Maryam's untimely deaths seem even more poignant.

The anger and bitterness that had eaten away at Zahir for six long years released its grip on his heart and was replaced by a new emotion that was unexpectedly fierce. Love—pure and uncomplicated—flooded through him, and he reached out and stroked Kazim's cheek with fingers that shook slightly.

Faisal's little son was an orphan, but he would never feel alone or unloved. He, Zahir, would make sure of that. Because of his stubborn pride he had left it too late to be reconciled with his brother, but he would love his nephew as if he were his own child. Kazim belonged in Qubbah, and nothing would prevent Zahir from taking him home.

His mind turned briefly to Faisal's second wife and he dismissed her with a shrug. Erin was an inconvenience he would have to deal with. For now he focused all his attention on his brother's son.

'He seems tall for a three-year-old,' he commented to the cook, who had settled her generous frame into an armchair by the fire.

'Oh, he is—and strong,' she agreed cheerfully. 'He's strong-willed too. Kazim's an adorable child, but he knows his own mind. Sometimes Erin struggles to cope with his temper tantrums, especially at bath-time.'

Zahir frowned. 'What do you mean—*struggles*? Does she lose her temper with him?'

Kazim was a sturdy toddler, but he had been left alone in the world since his father's death, totally dependent on Erin's care. Who *was* this woman Faisal had entrusted with his son? Erin had said that she loved Kazim but he, Zahir, was linked to Kazim by blood, and a wave of protectiveness swept through him.

'Heavens, no.' Alice shook her head. 'Erin is wonderfully patient with him. She really does think of him as her own child—and, after all, she's the only mother he's ever known.'

The cook's words were unwelcome, and Zahir's frown deepened, but when he glanced up his features were schooled into a disarming smile. 'I understand that Erin married my brother a year ago, but that she worked for him before that?'

'Yes. The master employed her as Kazim's nanny soon after he moved into Ingledean,' Alice confirmed, opening up like a flower beneath Zahir's full-on charm. 'She lived at the gate lodge with her foster parents, but when they retired and moved south to be near their son Erin moved in here. She always loved this house.' Alice's voice dropped. 'After Faisal died there was some unpleasant gossip in the village that Erin had persuaded him to marry her by promising to take care of Kazim because she wanted to inherit Ingledean.' She snorted. 'All rubbish, of course—Erin doesn't have a mercenary bone in her body—but some folk are so mean-minded, and they dug up all that about her past…'

The cook looked suddenly uncomfortable, and Zahir demanded sharply, 'What about her past?'

'Oh, it was nothing,' Alice assured him quickly. 'Erin had an unhappy childhood, and as a teenager she ended up in trouble with the law. It was a minor offence, I understand. I don't know much about it.' Alice trailed to a halt, clearly embarrassed that she had allowed her tongue to run away with her. 'What I do know is that Faisal trusted Erin,' she said firmly, as she got to her feet and threw a log on the fire. 'And although they might not have had a normal marriage, they were very fond of each other.'

In what way had his brother's marriage not been *normal*? Zahir wondered curiously. He wanted to force some more answers from the cook, but Alice was looking pink-cheeked and flustered, and with an effort he restrained his impatience. He would phone his personal assistant, Omran, as soon as possible, and instruct him to research Erin's background. He had grown up in a royal palace where intrigue and gossip were rife, but he knew from experience that even the wildest rumours often contained grains of truth. Omran's diligence was next to none, and if there were any skeletons in Faisal's widow's cupboard they would soon be revealed, he thought grimly.

He turned his attention back to Kazim, and this time his smile was genuine. 'I brought a present for you,' he told the little boy, his heart softening when Kazim's eyes lit up with excitement. 'It's a toy camel, just like the real camels that live in the desert. How would you like to come to my home in the desert and ride on one?'

Erin pushed open the library door to see Kazim staring at Zahir, utterly spellbound. Zahir was crouched low, so that his face was on a level with Kazim's, and Erin was instantly struck by the familial likeness between the man and the child. Kazim shared his uncle's Arabic colouring and silky black hair. An image filtered into her mind of the two of them astride a camel, Zahir's arms around Kazim as the animal carried them across golden sands.

The picture in her head was so real that she drew a sharp breath. Kazim's home was here at Ingledean, with her, she reminded herself, fighting the sudden surge of panic that gripped her. She turned to Alice, who was watching Zahir with a dreamy expression on her face that fuelled Erin's irritation. Okay, so the man looked like Lawrence of Arabia, and his voice was no longer cold and haughty but as warm and sensuous as molten syrup—but that was no reason to drool over him, she thought crossly.

'Erin—I got a camel.' Kazim finally noticed her and ran across the room, waving the toy excitedly at her. 'I'm going to ride on one—a *real* one,' he added emphatically, his brown eyes glowing with anticipation. 'Can we go to the desert *now*?'

Out of the mouths of babes! Erin managed to simultaneously smile at the toddler and glare at Zahir, who had straightened to his full height once more and dominated the room.

'Not today, darling,' she murmured. 'The desert is a long way from here.' She swung her gaze back to Zahir and gave him a cool smile that belied the frantic thudding of her heart.

'Gordon Straker was sensible to leave before the weather worsens. I suggest you do the same. I'm sure you would prefer not to be stranded in this "draughty monstrosity of a house,"' she added sweetly. 'Alice, will you take Kazim to the kitchen? It's time for his tea.'

'Oh—right.' Alice looked faintly startled at Erin's brisk tone, but held out her hand to Kazim and led him from the room.

The cook closed the door behind her, leaving Erin alone with Zahir, and her heart sank when she glanced at him and saw that his face had hardened, his eyes blazing with anger.

'You would begrudge me even five minutes with my brother's child?' he demanded harshly. 'Kazim is my flesh and blood—'

'I didn't know about you.' Erin quickly defended herself. 'Faisal told me that neither he nor his first wife had any family. You must understand that your appearance here today has been a shock.' She bit her lip, her thoughts whirling around her brain. 'When you say that Kazim has family in Qubbah— who are they, exactly?'

'My father…' Zahir paused; Erin seemed genuinely shocked that Faisal had a family. For some reason Faisal had not told her that he was a prince, nor that his son was heir to the throne of Qubbah, but for now he saw no reason to impart that information. 'My family have much power and influence in Qubbah,' he informed her. 'My father, Sheikh Kahlid, is eager to see his tenth grandson. My three sisters are married, and have children who are Kazim's cousins, and my father has six siblings who, together with their husbands and wives and children, make up a large extended family.

'Surely you must see that it would be better for Kazim to be brought up by his real family, by relatives who will love him, who can teach him of his heritage and culture and who want only the best for him?' he demanded impatiently when Erin stared at him, stunned into silence by the revelation that Kazim had a huge family in Qubbah.

Kazim was hers, she thought frantically, and no one could take him from her. Gordon Straker had said so. '*I* love him,' she said fiercely. 'I want what is best for him. And I don't think that carting him off to unfamiliar surroundings and a horde of people he's never met before would be good for him right now. You have to believe that my only concern is Kazim's welfare,' she continued, forcing herself to sound calm, although she felt anything but when Zahir was prowling the room, silent and menacing as a panther stalking its prey. 'I don't know the reason why Faisal was estranged from you and the rest of his family, but it must have been serious if he made no contact with you in six years. Kazim is a little boy who has lost both his parents, and he needs the security and stability of remaining here in the only home he has ever known. Perhaps when he is a bit older there could be some contact,' she offered hesitantly. You could visit…'

'I don't intend that my relationship with my brother's child will be confined to the occasional *visit*.' Zahir's icy scorn flayed her like a whip. 'Kazim belongs in Qubbah, with his blood family, and that is where I intend to take him—with or without your approval.'

'You can't.' Erin remembered Gordon Straker's warning not to allow Zahir to bully her, and she squared her shoulders, refusing to cower beneath his anger.

'The word *can't* is not one I am familiar with,' he informed her imperiously.

He wasn't joking, Erin realised shakily as she stared at his haughty expression. She had a feeling that no one had ever crossed Sheikh Zahir bin Kahlid al Muntassir in his life, and she did not relish being the first.

'Well, I'm afraid you're going to have to add it to your vocabulary,' she snapped. 'Kazim is legally my son, and I intend to follow Faisal's wishes and bring him up here in England. I can see that it would be good for Kazim to meet his relatives,' she conceded huskily, her voice faltering fractionally at the prospect of sharing the little boy with strangers who, if Zahir's attitude was anything to go by, would disapprove of her, 'and I understand your father's desire to see his grandson. For that reason I am prepared to allow him to visit Kazim.'

*Prepared to allow!* Outrage robbed Zahir temporarily of his ability to speak. No one *allowed* members of the ruling family of Qubbah to do anything. Their power was absolute in the tradition-bound kingdom. And as for being dictated to by a woman! Changes were slowly happening in his homeland, and he recognised that there would have to be many more if Qubbah did not want to be left behind as the world moved through the twenty-first century, but at present women had no status in Qubbah, and he was infuriated by Erin's assumption that he would meekly agree to her rules. Meek was not a word *ever* associated with Prince Zahir bin Kahlid al Muntassir!

He glanced out of the window at the gathering dusk and his jaw hardened. He did not have time to stand here arguing. He thought again of his father, remembering the look of devastation on his face when he had broken the news of Faisal's death. Kazim was a lifeline. He was possibly the only person who could lift the King from his despair. Nothing would prevent Zahir from taking the child home to the kingdom that he would one day rule.

'My nephew belongs in Qubbah,' he stated coldly as he crossed to the desk and reached into the inner pocket of his jacket. He could feel Erin's eyes on him, but he refused to look at her. He did not want to picture her with Faisal, did not want to admit to the corrosive jealousy that burned in his gut when he imagined them together. He was furious with himself that he could not banish the fantasy of making love to her so passionately that he drove all thoughts of his brother from her mind.

His unexpected desire for Erin was an inconvenience. Her legal status as Kazim's mother was a much bigger problem. But there was a simple solution. She had sounded convincing when she'd stated that she loved the child, but everything had its price—even love.

'We can deal with the situation in one of two ways,' he informed her coolly. 'The first is for me to gather the best lawyers I can find and fight you through the courts for custody of Kazim. The drawback is that any legal process takes time, and my father is eighty years old and desperate to meet his grandson as soon as possible. That is why I am prepared to offer you an extremely generous settlement in return for my brother's son.'

Now he looked at her, watched her beautiful grey eyes cloud with confusion as she slowly walked forward and took the cheque he held out to her. Her fingers trembled as she glanced down at it, and the colour drained from her face.

'I don't understand,' Erin said huskily. Her brain could not take in the number of noughts he had written after the figure, and she blinked to clear her vision. When she looked again she realised that she was not mistaken. Disbelief quickly gave way to disgust, and anger crashed through her, so violent in its intensity that that her whole body shook. 'Are you trying to *buy* Kazim?'

'I am offering you a chance to resume your life without the responsibilities of caring for a child who is not yours,' Zahir replied with deadly calm—in direct contrast to the fury flashing in her eyes. 'You are young and extraordinarily beautiful,' he observed clinically, his voice devoid of emotion. 'And, since my brother's death, single.' Although he would bet his personal fortune that she would not remain so for long, he thought grimly, watching the faint tremor of her lower lip and imagining the velvet softness of her mouth beneath his. 'I imagine that dating with a toddler in tow could prove rather…inhibiting,' he drawled sardonically.

'I have no intention of dating anyone,' Erin choked, still reeling from his description of her as beautiful. Astounding as it seemed, the Sheikh appeared to find her attractive—but from the coldness of his tone he clearly resented his awareness of her. 'I haven't even thought about anything like that…' Kazim was her world, and there was no room in her heart for anyone but him.

'Perhaps not yet,' Zahir conceded. 'It *is* only three weeks since my brother died. But at some point you will want to satisfy your sexual urges. I would guess that you possess a deeply sensual nature,' he remarked, in that same coldly clinical tone that was so at odds with the heat in his gaze as he trailed a blatantly appreciative path down her body. 'Kazim will become an encumbrance, and I refuse to allow him to spend his childhood forced to vie for your attention with your latest lover.'

'I don't want a lover!' Erin shook her head wildly, her temper heating to boiling point.

Zahir made her sound like a rampant nymphomaniac, with his talk about her sensual nature and needing to satisfy her sexual urges. Little did he know! She was about as sensual as a limp lettuce, and she had never experienced the faintest urge to have sex with any man—*until today*, a voice in her head taunted. She ignored it and allowed her anger to build as she dwelled on his disgusting offer to buy Kazim from her. She stared down at the cheque, and the row of scrawled noughts, and felt sick.

'Get out!' she breathed as she ripped the cheque into pieces with controlled savagery. 'Kazim is not for sale.'

Zahir showed no reaction, merely stood surveying her disdainfully from beneath raised brows, his lip curled in a derisive smile that snapped her control so that she flung the pieces of cheque at him. 'How *dare* you come into *my* house and demand that I hand you *my* child?' She emphasised each word by jabbing her finger into Zahir's chest, uncaring that he towered menacingly over her. 'Faisal begged me to adopt his son, and now I know why. You are an arrogant, overbearing bully, and I will do everything possible to prevent you from having *any* role in Kazim's life.'

'*Enough!*' The authority in Zahir's icy command sliced through her furious tirade, and she gasped when he seized her hand, which was still raised to his chest, and jerked her so that her body slammed hard up against his. 'You will not talk to me in that insolent tone.'

'I will talk to you in whatever tone I like, and there's not a damn thing you can do about it.'

Zahir fought to control the murderous rage coursing through him. Never in his life had he been so insulted. He couldn't believe Erin had actually prodded him. If she had been a man, retribution would have been swift and deadly. But she was a woman—a woman who needed a few lessons in respect.

She was glaring up at him, her grey eyes stormy and her cheeks stained with angry colour. Her wild red curls formed a fiery halo around her face and he pictured her lying beneath him, flushed and furious, daring him to kiss her…

With a savage oath he lowered his head, forcing her slender neck back as he captured her mouth in a kiss that sought to dominate and subjugate her to his will. This had been building from the moment she had stared at him across the library and he had recognised the undisguised hunger in her eyes. Sexual attraction at its most primitive—and they were both caught in its spell.

'No!' Erin's cry of protest was lost beneath the punishing force of Zahir's lips as he ground them against hers.

How *dared* he kiss her? How dared he slide his arm around her waist and drag her even closer against the rock-hard wall of his muscular chest? His other hand moved up to cup her nape and angle her head so that he could plunder her mouth with humiliating ease. Beneath his civilised veneer Zahir bin Kahlid al Muntassir was a barbarian: frighteningly powerful and supremely masculine. His arms felt like steel bands holding her fast, and when he forced his tongue between her lips she moaned and tried to turn her head to evade his ruthless assault.

Her attempts to resist him were futile. The blows she rained on him with her bunched fists had no impact. Finally she laid her hands flat on his chest, unable to fight him any more. He must have sensed her submission, because he eased the pressure of his lips a fraction and the stroke of his tongue inside her mouth became a slow, sensual exploration.

Suddenly each of her senses seemed acutely alive. She

could feel the heat of his body through his fine silk shirt, and the mingled scents of his cologne and male pheromones caused a curious weakness in her limbs. Her anger was dissipating, giving way to another emotion she had never experienced before: a slow, insidious excitement that unlocked her taut muscles so that she stopped trying to pull away from him and instead melted into him.

Her eyes flew open in shock when she felt the hard ridge of his arousal push insistently against her belly. What was the matter with her? she wondered, appalled at her shaming weakness. Zahir was a tyrant—a man used to always having his own way, according to Gordon Straker. She despised his arrogance. But the pressure of his hand on her spine was forcing her body into intimate contact with his, and nothing else seemed to matter except that he should carry on kissing her.

She felt his hand slide down to her bottom and then round, over her hip, smoothing a tantalising path up to her ribcage, where it came to rest just below her breast. Heat flooded through her veins and she felt her breasts swell, felt her nipples tighten in anticipation beneath her tee shirt. He only had to move his hand a little further… In an agony of excitement she pressed closer to him, her body trembling with desire.

Nothing existed but the firm pressure of his mouth on hers, the sensual sweep of his tongue and the warm weight of his hand resting so close to where she wanted him to touch her. Lost in this new world of sensory pleasure, she shifted closer still, rubbed her pelvis against his—and then suddenly, shockingly, he wrenched his mouth from hers, his fingers biting into her flesh as he thrust her from him.

The ensuing silence throbbed with a sexual tension that was almost tangible, and for a few mad seconds Erin wished he would draw her back into his arms and kiss her again and again, until they were both mindless with wanting. But then he spoke and she wished instead that she could curl up and die of humiliation.

'I see that my assessment of your nature was spot-on,' he drawled in a hatefully sardonic tone. 'My brother has been in his grave barely three weeks and yet you're already clearly sexually frustrated. How long, I wonder, will it be before you invite a steady stream of boyfriends into the house? And what sort of care will Kazim receive then, when you are too busy for him?'

'I want you to leave,' Erin said tightly, her chest heaving as she fought to drag oxygen into her lungs.

She could not bring herself to look at him. It was pointless trying to defend herself—pointless to explain that she'd never had a proper boyfriend in all her twenty-two years. Zahir clearly believed she was the Mata Hari of the Yorkshire Moors, and after the shameful way she had responded to him she couldn't really blame him.

Shaking with reaction, she yanked open the library door and stood aside for Zahir to pass—then gasped when he caught hold of her arm and slammed the door shut again, the blaze of anger in his eyes filling her with trepidation.

'I came here to collect my brother's child, and I'm not going anywhere without him,' he warned her savagely.

'So what are you going to do? Kidnap him? Take him from me by force?' Erin demanded shakily.

Ingledean was eight miles from the nearest village, and she had always loved its remoteness, but Zahir was strong and powerful and she and Alice would be no match for him if he chose to snatch Kazim.

'If you don't leave now I'll call the police,' she told him with a bravado she did not feel, aware even as she spoke of the emptiness of her threat. He could carry Kazim out to his car, parked on the driveway, and disappear into the dusk before the local constable even had cycled out from the village. 'You say you want what is best for Kazim, but how can scaring him out of his wits be good for him?'

'Of course I do not mean to scare him,' Zahir snapped impatiently. But her words had hit a chord, and he stared at her, his conscience prickling when he glimpsed the fear in her eyes.

He had not meant to lose his temper, and he was furious with himself for his loss of control. He shouldn't have kissed her like that—but she had made him angrier than he could ever remember, and she had responded to him, damn it. He could still taste her, could remember that moment of scalding sweetness when she had stopped fighting him and parted her lips beneath his while her body relaxed into him so that her soft breasts had pressed against his chest.

With a muttered curse he swung away from her and raked his hand through his hair. She was his brother's widow, he reminded himself grimly, and out of respect for Faisal she was off-limits.

'I have no intention of taking my nephew away from you,' he growled. He'd witnessed how the little boy had clung to Erin when he had injured himself, and in all honesty he knew he could not separate Kazim from the woman he regarded as his mother.

'You don't?' Erin murmured dazedly, a little of her tension draining away. A moment ago he'd told her that he would not leave without Kazim.

'No.' Zahir's jaw tightened. The last thing he wanted was

to take this woman who was playing havoc with his hormones back to his homeland, but he had no choice. 'I appreciate that he needs you, and for that reason it's clear that you will have to come to Qubbah too.'

He was deadly serious, Erin realised when she stared at him and recognised the determined gleam in his eyes. 'I don't think you understand,' she began. 'I'm not going to Qubbah or anywhere else with you, and neither is Kazim…'

'It is *you* who does not understand,' Zahir snapped coldly. 'My father is desperate to see his grandson.'

'I told you—your father is welcome to visit Kazim whenever he likes,' Erin said defensively, flushing beneath Zahir's hard stare.

'The journey would kill him.' He ignored her faint gasp. 'Two months ago my father contracted a virus that attacked his heart. He has been prescribed medication to control the condition and hopefully prevent full heart failure, but he has to rest as much as possible, and his doctors give him oxygen to reduce any strain on his heart. A long flight is out of the question,' Zahir said harshly. 'The only solution is for you to accompany Kazim to Qubbah. And, to be frank, I don't have much time to waste arguing with you,' he added in a warning tone when she opened her mouth to protest. 'My father longed to be reconciled with Faisal, and he was devastated by the news of his death. He is an old man, and his life is in the balance,' he added gruffly. 'All he wants is to see his grandson—Faisal's son. And you want to deny him that one simple joy.'

Erin bit her lip, startled by the raw emotion in Zahir's voice. Guilt tugged at her conscience. She more than most people understood the importance of family ties. All her life she had longed to be part of a family, and even though her mother had been sadly lacking in any parenting skills, she had still been devastated by the death of her only blood relative.

Supposing the elderly Sheikh died without ever seeing Kazim? From the sound of it Zahir's father had loved Faisal, had hoped to be reconciled with him, and according to Zahir he was desperate to meet his little grandson. And what about Kazim? she thought fretfully. Would a court battle with Zahir for custody really be in the little boy's best interests? And how would Kazim feel if he one day discovered that she had prevented him from meeting his grandfather?

The truth was she had a duty to give Kazim the opportunity to meet his family in Qubbah, she acknowledged reluctantly. She could not possibly allow Zahir to take Kazim—she would have to go too. But the prospect of travelling halfway around the world with Faisal's disturbingly sexy brother filled her with unease.

What if he tried to kiss her again? She would not respond, of course. He had taken her by surprise earlier, that was all. But she had a feeling that Zahir bin Kahlid al Muntassir was used to women jumping whenever he clicked his fingers, and she would have to make it clear that she was neither available nor interested in him. Her eyes strayed to his mouth and her stomach lurched as she recalled the sensual pleasure of his kiss, the way his warm, firm lips had parted hers with a masterful intent that had demolished her resistance. Definitely not interested, she told herself sharply, her heart jerking unevenly when their eyes met and held and a bolt of white-hot awareness flashed between them.

Faisal had been a kind, gentle man, but she detected neither quality in his brother. Common sense warned her that Zahir, with his stunning looks and brooding sensuality, was out of her league, but for some reason her body hadn't got the message, and she blushed scarlet when she followed his amused gaze and saw that her nipples were jutting provocatively beneath her tee shirt.

Desperate to distract his attention, she crossed her arms over her chest and voiced the question that had been gnawing in her brain since Gordon Straker's shocking announcement that Zahir was Faisal's brother. 'Why was Faisal estranged from you and the rest of his family?'

Zahir was silent for so long that she risked another glance at him, and was startled by the hardness of his expression. 'He married a woman who had not been chosen for him,' he replied at last. 'Faisal was engaged to the daughter of an influential family in Qubbah, but before his wedding he eloped with another woman and brought great shame to his family.'

'When you say that his fiancée had been chosen for him, do you mean that it was an arranged marriage?' Erin queried, shocked. 'Isn't that a rather outdated tradition?'

'It is the tradition in Qubbah,' Zahir informed her coldly. 'My father had selected a number of potential brides, and Faisal chose one of them.'

'But he didn't love her,' Erin said, her voice ringing with conviction. 'He loved Maryam. He talked about her all the time, and I know that her death left him heartbroken. Why did Faisal have to elope with her? Why couldn't he have married her and stayed in Qubbah?'

'Because Maryam was promised to another man,' Zahir said flatly, and something in his tone caused Erin to stare at him curiously.

'Another arranged marriage?' she guessed. 'But Maryam

didn't love the man she was expected to marry—she was in love with Faisal. It's like something from the Dark Ages. Surely your father wanted his son to be happy? Why couldn't he have relented and allowed Faisal and Maryam to be together?'

'Because it would have been an unforgivable insult to his fiancée and her family,' Zahir explained harshly, his eyes narrowing when he noted Erin's disapproving expression. 'Things are done differently in my country. I don't expect you to understand,' he told her dismissively.

'You're right—I don't understand,' Erin told him hotly. 'I believe that the only reason two people should marry is because they love each other, as Faisal and Maryam did. Yet it sounds as though they were hounded out of Qubbah like criminals…'

'They were not,' Zahir snapped furiously. 'My father is not some cruel despot. But he is bound by his duty to the kingdom. He was torn…' He shook his head, belatedly remembering that Erin had no idea his father was the King of Qubbah.

The tense silence was shattered by the ring of his mobile phone. It was a welcome interruption, and he answered the call, listened intently, and then barked a few terse instructions in Arabic before turning back to Erin. 'My driver has been following the weather reports and says that more snow is forecast. We will have to leave immediately. I cannot risk the possibility of being stranded here for days,' he added impatiently, when Erin gaped at him.

'You can't expect us to come with you *now*?' she faltered, tension making her voice sharp as it dawned on her that Zahir expected exactly that. 'I can see that because your father is ill I'll have to bring Kazim to Qubbah for a short visit, but not *today*! The idea is ridiculous. I'd have to pack. And it's late. In a couple of hours it'll be Kazim's bedtime…'

'He can sleep on the plane,' Zahir informed her coolly. 'We'll be travelling on my private jet, and one of the bedrooms on board has already been prepared for him. It is not necessary for you to bring anything for him. He has clothes and toys, everything he could possibly want, in Qubbah. Everything is taken care of. You can quickly pack your own personal possessions if you wish,' he added graciously. 'And may I suggest you change into a more suitable outfit to travel in.' His eyes briefly skimmed her faded jeans with such a disdainful expression that Erin itched to slap him. 'Something lightweight—it is considerably hotter in Qubbah than here.'

He was the most arrogant, overstuffed...Erin ran out of adjectives and glared at him with such heated fury that he should have fried on the spot. 'Now, look here...'

Behind her the library door creaked open. She swung round, breathing hard, and forced a smile when Kazim peeped into the room.

'Hey, have you had your tea? I'd better come and run your bath.'

Bathtime had become something of a battlefield lately, and Kazim shook his head mutinously. He seemed fascinated by Zahir, and although he was usually shy with people he did not know, he trotted across the room and grinned when his uncle swung him into his arms.

'Instead of a bath, how would you like to fly on my plane, Kazim?'

The little boy's eyes widened and he nodded his head eagerly. 'A real plane?'

'Sure it's a real plane. It's a jet, and it will take us all the way to the desert—'

'Hold on a minute,' Erin interrupted in a fierce whisper

meant for Zahir's ears only. 'I'm not convinced it's a good
idea for Kazim to travel tonight.' She wasn't convinced that
she should take him to Qubbah at all, but Zahir was like a bull-
dozer, flattening anything that got in his way and trampling
on her misgivings with arrogant disregard.

Zahir's eyes hardened on her before he smiled at the child
in his arms. 'Kazim wants to come with me—don't you?' he
prompted the toddler lightly. 'But if Erin doesn't want to
come, just you and me can go—how about that?'

Erin's heart missed a beat when Kazim rested his head on
his uncle's shoulder. He appeared to be completely dazzled by
Zahir—and he was not the only one, she acknowledged grimly
as she recalled those few moments when he had crushed her
against his chest and she had inhaled his tantalising male scent.

'Erin's coming on the plane too,' Kazim announced firmly,
grinning at her from his high vantage point in Zahir's arms.

Some of Erin's tension left her. Zahir might be Superman
in Kazim's eyes, but he still needed her, and she smiled back
at him, her smile fading as she glared at Zahir. 'That was a
dirty, low-down trick, and you know it,' she said furiously.

He shrugged uninterestedly. 'I'll play dirty if I have to, and
you would be wise to remember that,' he advised her coldly.

The implied threat in his voice sent a shaft of fear
through her.

He sauntered over to the door, still holding Kazim. 'Come,
Kazim, let's go and play with your toys while Erin packs.' He
laughed at the toddler's excited nod, but his expression was
deadly serious when he looked back at Erin. 'You have half
an hour,' he drawled, glancing at his watch. 'I suggest you get
a move on—or risk being left behind.'

# CHAPTER THREE

IT HAD stopped snowing when they left Ingledean. The evening air was crisp and cold and Erin shivered in the cream linen skirt and jacket that she had changed into for the journey. Zahir had warned her that it would be hot in Qubbah and she only hoped he was right.

At least she no longer looked like a 'menial domestic', she thought, recalling his scathing description of her when he had first learned that she was Faisal's widow. Stung by his remarks, she had taken time with her appearance and had teamed her suit with a pale blue silk blouse, swept her unruly curls into a knot on top of her head and even added a touch of make-up—just a soft taupe shadow on her eyelids and pink gloss on her lips.

She had felt supremely self-conscious when she'd walked down the stairs to where he's been waiting in the hall with Kazim, and the flare of sexual heat in his eyes had caused her heart to jerk painfully beneath her ribs.

Her doubts about taking Kazim to visit his family in Qubbah were intensifying by the minute, but she seemed to have little choice. Zahir had swept into their lives with the force of a tornado and she was still reeling from his impact.

She and Kazim would be back at Ingledean soon, she re-assured herself as the car swung out of the drive, and she turned her head for one last glimpse of the house that was the only real home she had ever known. She loved Ingledean. The wild beauty of the surrounding moors was a stark contrast to the soulless concrete tower block where she had grown up.

If Zahir's father was as ill as he'd described, then surely he would not want them to make a prolonged visit? She would stay in Qubbah long enough for Kazim to meet his grandfa-ther and other relatives, and then she would bring him home to Yorkshire.

Kazim chattered non-stop on the drive to the airport, and his excitement grew as they boarded Zahir's private plane. Erin felt as though she had stepped into another world when she glanced around the luxurious cabin. Instead of rows of tightly packed seats there were large cream leather sofas and a plush velvet carpet. The discreet lighting created an ambience of refined luxury, and the cabin crew—two impos-sibly beautiful stewardesses—were charmingly attentive. Particularly towards Zahir, she noted sourly. It was little wonder that he was so arrogant when everyone he came into contact with seemed to hang on his every word. But perhaps being surrounded by yes-men—and women—was one of the perks of being incredibly wealthy.

She'd known that Faisal was well off, but he had lived simply and she had never given a thought to his fortune. Now she was forced to acknowledge that Kazim's family were millionaires—probably billionaires, she amended, as she debated the likelihood of the fitments in the bathroom being solid gold. She felt a churning sensation in the pit of her stomach. Money and power went hand in hand, and she could not forget Zahir's threat that he would hire the best lawyers and fight for custody of his nephew. But surely he wouldn't do so now that she had agreed to bring Kazim to Qubbah?

Once they were in the air Kazim quickly became bored and fretful, despite Erin's attempts to entertain him. He was over-tired, and she was relieved when one of the stewardesses escorted them to a bedroom at the rear of the plane, where he fell asleep as soon as his head touched the pillow. She had assumed that Zahir would continue working on his laptop, as he had done since they had taken off, but to her consternation he was waiting for her when she returned to the main cabin, and indicated that she should join him on the sofa.

'Champagne?'

He handed her a glass without waiting for her to reply and settled next to her, stretching his long legs out in front of him and tucking his arms behind his head so that she was acutely conscious of his lean, powerful body. She could make out the hard ridges of his abdominal muscles beneath the silk shirt, and guessed that the dark hairs revealed where he had dis-carded his tie and unfastened the top couple of buttons covered his broad chest. The subtle tang of his cologne teased her senses…

In a desperate attempt to hide the effect he was having on her she took a gulp of champagne—and choked as the bubbles hit the back of her throat.

Zahir was watching her. He appeared relaxed as he sipped his own champagne, but his eyes were hooded, so that she had no idea what he was thinking. His next words threw her completely.

'Tell me, Erin, why exactly did you marry my brother?'

'What do you mean?' She set her glass down on the onyx table-top with an unsteady hand. It was an innocuous-sounding question, but she remembered the solicitor Gordon Straker's warning to be on her guard.

Zahir's dark eyes were coolly assessing as he said, 'I mean, did you know Faisal was dying before you became his wife?'

If only she knew where this was leading! 'I knew he was ill. He was undergoing tests.' That much was true; she saw no reason to explain that Faisal had been pessimistic about his prognosis right from the beginning. 'Why do you ask?'

'I'm curious to understand your motives. While you were packing I took a look around Ingledean House, and I saw that the master bedroom—which still contains many of Faisal's belongings—is on the third floor, but that you occupy a room next to the nursery. It's customary for a married couple to sleep together—so why didn't you and Faisal share a room?'

The silence stretched between them before Erin replied icily, 'I really don't think that's any of your business.'

'Oh, I think it is,' Zahir argued, in a dangerously soft tone that sent a shiver down Erin's spine. 'The cook intimated to me that your marriage to my brother was not "normal". She also revealed that there had been gossip in the village about your motives for marrying a wealthy man who was obviously seriously ill.'

He waited for Erin to absorb his words, noting how the colour had drained from her face. She looked very young, and that air of innocence was very convincing. It was easy to see how she had fooled Faisal three years ago, when he had been a grieving widower with a baby son. Hell, she had almost fooled *him*, Zahir mused grimly. But the information his personal assistant had emailed him after running a data check revealed things about her that he was sure his brother had known nothing about. Things like a criminal record for shoplifting, and details of a life that had been spiralling out of control—until she had been fostered by an elderly couple who had taken her to their home in the caretaker's cottage in the grounds of Ingledean House.

There she had managed to catch up on her education, and had trained as a nanny, but more controversy had followed with her first job, looking after the children of a respected barrister and land-owner at his country estate on the outskirts of York. Omran had unearthed talk of an affair between Erin and Giles Fitzroy. It was rumoured that she had pursued her wealthy employer in the hope that he would leave his wife for her, but that eventually Fitzroy had come to his senses and dismissed her. Soon after that Faisal had bought Ingledean and taken Erin on as Kazim's nanny.

His brother must have seemed like a gift from the gods, Zahir thought darkly—a rich man without the complication of a wife. Erin had no doubt seized the opportunity to ingratiate herself with Faisal and his motherless son.

'Shall I tell you what I think?' he queried silkily, when Erin did not reply. 'I suspect that your marriage to Faisal was not a conventional one, and the fact that you occupied separate bedrooms reinforces that belief. I also think it's possible that you deliberately coerced my brother into marrying you.' He paused, his eyes as dark and cold as bottomless pools.

'Faisal was estranged from his family and he was desperate to ensure that Kazim would be well cared for after his death. I'm convinced that when you learned of Faisal's illness you played on the vulnerable emotions of a dying man and persuaded him to marry you by promising to care for Kazim. What my brother did not realise,' Zahir continued harshly, 'was that you were prepared to go to almost any lengths to gain Ingledean House and a substantial fortune—including being saddled with a small child. But if I can prove that your motives for adopting my nephew were not as altruistic as Faisal believed, I'm certain that a judge will look favourably on my custody claim of Kazim.'

'But you're wrong,' Erin gasped, so shocked by his accusations that she could barely utter the denial. 'The only reason I adopted Kazim is because I adore him. Ingledean had nothing to do with it—'

She broke off, feeling sick with fear at Zahir's threat to fight for Kazim. Alice had known, of course, that her marriage to Faisal had been in name only and that she had married him for Kazim's sake. But if Alice unwittingly revealed news to Zahir, could it strengthen his case in a court battle over Kazim? And *would* a judge question her motives for marrying a wealthy, dying man and decide that it would be better for Kazim to be brought up by his uncle? That was something she simply could not risk.

'I married your brother for love,' she stated fiercely, but the open derision in Zahir's expression prompted her to lie to him. 'Alice was mistaken. I assure you our marriage was completely "normal" in every sense.'

And let him prove otherwise, she thought shakily, turning away from his penetrating gaze. At least her statement that she had married for love was the truth. But it had been her love for Kazim, whom Faisal had led her to believe would be all alone in the world, which had made her agree to his proposal.

She could not bear to remain sitting with Zahir now that she knew he held such a disgusting opinion of her, and with a mumbled excuse that she wanted to check on Kazim she jumped to her feet and stumbled towards the bedroom.

The little boy was sleeping soundly, and she curled up on the sofa next to the bed and watched him, feeling the familiar surge of love flood through her. She studied him, angelic in sleep, with his mass of black hair and his long eyelashes that made dark crescents on his velvet-soft cheeks. He was hers. Faisal had entrusted him to her and she would never let him go, she vowed.

But she could not dismiss her terror that Zahir might win a custody battle, and she drifted into a fitful sleep where her dreams were haunted by him wrenching Kazim from her arms.

'Look Erin—camels!' Kazim cried several hours later as he peered out of the window of the luxury four-by-four that was speeding them across the desert. He pointed excitedly at the group of camels plodding over a distant sand dune, led by a group of tribesmen. 'See them? Can we ride on camels, Zahir?' he asked breathlessly.

'Not those ones,' Zahir replied in his deep, melodious voice that, to Erin's chagrin, had the annoying effect of bringing her skin out in goosebumps. 'But I promise that as soon as we reach my home I will arrange to take you for a ride on the friendliest camel I can find. Okay?'

Kazim nodded fervently and beamed at Zahir. Her son was suffering from a serious case of hero-worship, Erin acknowledged dismally, recalling how she had woken at dawn, as the plane began its descent, and discovered that Kazim was already awake, sitting on Zahir's lap while they watched the sun rise over the desert. It was clear that a bond had already been forged between the little boy and his uncle, and Erin despised herself for feeling jealous. Kazim was her world, and she didn't want to share him with anyone, but she could not deny him the chance to meet his family. This trip was turning into a nightmare and she couldn't wait for it to be over.

She stared out at the endless expanse of golden sand and her spirits plummeted further. There was nothing on the horizon: no sign of a village or a house, not even a tree—just sand and sky, shimmering in the heat haze.

'I can't imagine why anyone would want to live in this baking wilderness,' she muttered. She glanced at her watch and realised that it was half an hour since they had left the town and set off across the desert. 'Are we *anywhere* near our destination?'

'The desert is the most beautiful place in the world,' Zahir snapped coldly, glowering at her. 'Kazim will love it. You should be able to see the walls of the fortress in another ten minutes.'

'The fort…? Just where are you taking us?'

Her feeling of unease had grown from the moment Zahir's jet had landed in Qubbah and she'd seen the fleet of vehicles lined up on the runway, flags fluttering on their bonnets. Zahir had said that his family were influential in Qubbah, but she'd been startled when they had descended the plane's steps and several Arab men, whom she'd guessed were members of his staff, had immediately leapt from the cars and bowed to him. Anyone would think he was royalty, the way people seemed to worship the ground he walked on.

With a heavy sigh she resumed her contemplation of the barren landscape, relief flooding through her when she spied the distant outline of walls and high towers. But her relief gave way to sheer astonishment ten minutes later, when they drove through the huge arched gateway of what was clearly an ancient fortress and then down a mile-long, sweeping driveway, lined on either side by palm trees, before halting outside the most amazing building she had ever seen.

She turned her shocked gaze on Zahir. 'You're not seriously telling me you live here?' she croaked, staring, awestruck, at the countless marble steps gleaming beneath the brilliant glare of the sun, leading up to a vast white stone residence that resembled a fantasy Arabian palace, with gold-topped turrets and tall, graceful pillars lining the entrance.

Zahir had already released Kazim's seat belt and lifted him from his child seat. He spared Erin a brief glance as someone opened the car door. 'This is my home—welcome to the Palace of the Falcon,' he murmured coolly. He stepped out of the car with Kazim in his arms, and a man wearing robes immediately bowed his head in greeting.

'Your Highness.'

Erin scrambled to follow Zahir, and emerged from the car flushed and wild-eyed. What did the man mean—*Your Highness?* she wondered frantically.

After the cool interior of the air-conditioned car the heat hit her as though she had walked into a furnace, and while Zahir looked cool and urbane, in his pale grey designer suit, she knew that her skirt was badly creased and she did not look nearly so elegant.

'Who *are* you?' she breathed, desperately trying to keep up with him as he strode up the steps. But Zahir ignored her and swept through the magnificent arched doorway into a vast entrance hall. There, the white marble floor and huge pillars contrasted with the décor of red and gold, creating a look of such opulence that Erin stopped dead and stared open-mouthed before stumbling after him. 'Zahir!'

'You must walk behind the Prince.' The man who had opened the car door was following close behind her, and as she made to run and catch up with Zahir he put a restraining hand on her arm. 'And you are not permitted to address His Royal Highness. You must only speak if he addresses you.'

'But…' Erin shook her head, feeling as though she had landed on another planet. 'What do you mean? Zahir isn't a prince—is he?' She faltered, flushing beneath the man's curious stare.

'He is most certainly a prince—the second son of our eminent ruler, His Royal Highness King Kahlid,' the man informed her, his expression faintly scornful as he took in her pink cheeks and the vivid curls that had escaped the pins on top of her head and now clustered around her hot face. 'My name is Omran. I am Prince Zahir's personal assistant.'

'Second son?' Erin parroted. 'You mean Faisal was a prince too?'

'He was the King's firstborn son, and heir to the Kingdom of Qubbah,' Omran confirmed. 'Under our ancient laws, when the King dies only his eldest son can rule Qubbah.'

'But Faisal is dead,' Erin said tremulously. She remembered Zahir's words about his father being elderly. 'What will happen when King Kahlid dies now that Faisal can't take his place?'

'The crown will pass to Prince Faisal's eldest son,' Omran said simply. 'Prince Kazim will one day rule the kingdom. That is why Prince Zahir was dispatched to England to bring the child to Qubbah.'

They were walking along a seemingly endless corridor lined with yet more pillars, which seemed to Erin to loom up to the ceiling like the bars of a prison. She could feel her heart thudding painfully in her chest as Omran's words slowly sank in. 'But Kazim is three years old—he's little more than a baby. And he doesn't belong here,' she told Omran desperately. 'His home is in England—with me.'

Omran frowned and shook his head. 'The young Prince belongs here now. It is the King's word,' he said, with a finality that filled Erin with terror.

She could see Zahir striding on ahead, carrying Kazim away from her. With a cry she jerked her arm from Omran's grasp and flew along the corridor, ignoring his terse warning that she was not permitted to chase after His Royal Highness. She tore up another flight of marble stairs, following the route Zahir had taken, and stumbled, panting and breathless, into a room that appeared at first sight to be an Aladdin's Cave of toys.

Zahir had set Kazim down, and the toddler was now running around the room, his eyes huge with excitement as he climbed into a toy racing car and then sped over to a model train set that ran the full length of one wall.

'I can make the trains work. See! When I push the button they go!'

'That's fantastic, darling. Aren't you lucky to have so many toys to play with while we stay here?'

Erin forced a smile for the overawed little boy, but her eyes flashed with fury as she turned to face Zahir. She recalled how he had warned her at Ingledean that he would play dirty if necessary, and a mixture of fear and anger churned inside her.

'What is this?' She glanced around at the array of toys. 'Your disgusting attempt to *bribe* a little boy?' she demanded scornfully. Zahir's personal assistant was hovering in the doorway, and her heart lurched as she remembered his astounding statement that Kazim was heir to the throne of Qubbah. 'You lied to me,' she accused Zahir furiously, ignoring the warning glint in his eyes. 'I don't care if you are a *prince*, you're also the biggest louse ever to walk this earth—and I hope you don't expect me to bow and scrape to you, because I won't!'

From a corner of the room came an audible gasp, and she swung round to see a young woman dressed in traditional robes staring at her with a look of undisguised horror on her pretty face.

'This is Bisma, who will be Kazim's nanny,' Zahir said tightly. His face was a taut mask of fury, and Erin's spurt of angry defiance wavered when he gripped her arm and dragged her over to the door. 'I will escort Kazim's stepmother to her room.' He addressed Bisma in English, and the young woman nodded and smiled faintly, clearly still shocked that Erin had shown such disrespect to a member of the royal family. 'We will leave you so that you and Kazim can become acquainted.'

To Erin's relief Bisma replied in perfect English. 'Of course, sire. I will let Prince Kazim explore the nursery, and then give him his lunch—if you wish me to,' she added hesitantly, when Erin opened her mouth to argue that Kazim was *her* responsibility.

Before she could comment, Zahir tightened his hold on her arm and tugged her forcefully out of the room.

Omran was hovering in the corridor and hurried forwards. 'Your Highness, permit me to show…' He hesitated, as if he was unsure of how to refer to Erin, and she detected a barely disguised insolence behind his unctuous smile. 'Erin to her quarters.'

This time Zahir replied in Arabic, but it was clear from his tone that he was dismissing his personal assistant, and judging from the shadow of resentment that crossed Omran's features he did not like it—or her—Erin was sure.

Zahir's staff were the least of her problems, she acknowledged, as he frogmarched her a short way along the corridor and into another room. At a quick glance she saw it was as sumptuously furnished as the rest of the palace. It was dominated by a large bed draped with a satin bedspread and scattered with silk cushions in rich shades of gold and peacock-blue.

Zahir gave her no time to admire the bedroom before he spun her round to face him and finally released her wrist. One look at his hard face told Erin he was still seething, and common sense dictated that she should try and defuse the situation, but her own temper was at boiling point and the contemptuous curl of his lip was the final straw.

'Brute,' she snapped, rubbing the red marks around her wrist. 'Why don't you pick on someone your own size?'

'One day that disrespectful tongue of yours is going to get you into a lot of trouble,' he said silkily, advancing menacingly towards her so that she backed away—until her legs met the end of the bed and she had nowhere else to go. 'Do you know what the punishment is for insulting a member of the Royal House of Qubbah?'

He towered over her, dark and dangerous, watching her intently with no hint of warmth in his black eyes. Erin could feel her heart jerk erratically in her chest, and suddenly she was fourteen again, her back pressed against the wall in an alley next to the care home, while a group of older girls edged closer…

*'I told you to bring me the new Wild Boys CD,' Terri, the ringleader said nastily. 'Why haven't you, Erin?'*

*'I don't have any money to buy a CD.'*

*A laugh went around the group and Terri smiled unpleasantly. 'Who said anything about buying it?' she taunted. 'You should have nicked it, you silly little cow. You need to learn what happens to people who don't do as they're told.'*

*The teenager struck without warning, hitting Erin in the*

*stomach with her clenched fist. Erin buckled with the intensity of the pain and fell to her knees as the crowd of girls moved in. She curled up in a ball and covered her face with her arms, just as she had learned to do when her mother had taken her drug-fuelled frustrations out on her.*

Keep your head down and it will be over more quickly— that had been one of the golden rules of her childhood. But now she blinked and glanced around the room—at Zahir— and the memory faded. She wasn't a scared adolescent any more; she was a mother, fighting for her child, and she threw her head back and glared at Zahir.

'So what are you going to do—hit me?' she demanded scornfully.

'I have never struck a woman in my life,' he snapped, sounding so genuinely shocked at the suggestion that Erin's eyes flew to his face.

She stared helplessly at his beautiful, sensual mouth and the razor-sharp lines of his cheekbones, and heat seeped through her veins. An unbidden memory of how he had kissed her in the library at Ingledean filled her mind. She groaned silently, hating herself for her weakness where he was concerned. Even the realisation that he believed her to be a gold-digger who had married his brother for money did not prevent her longing for him to kiss her again. The atmosphere between them had changed imperceptibly from anger to something far more dangerous. The air crackled with static electricity, and she saw Zahir's jaw clench as if he too was waging a violent internal battle.

'I did not lie to you,' he growled.

'No, you just conveniently forgot to mention that you are a royal prince, or that under Qubbah's laws Kazim is next in line to rule the kingdom. Well, I'm sorry to disappoint you,' Erin said sweetly, 'but once Kazim has met your father I'm taking him home. When he's eighteen he can decide whether or not he wants to take up his position as the next King. Until then he's going to enjoy a normal upbringing…'

'With a woman who tricked his father into marrying her so that she could inherit a house and a huge fortune,' Zahir finished grimly.

'*I did not trick Faisal*. He asked me to marry him and, as I've already told you, he begged me to adopt Kazim. I have had more than enough of your outrageous insults,' she muttered, trying to edge past him and failing when his big, muscle-packed body barred her way. 'I want to leave as soon as it can be arranged.'

'Suits me!' Zahir reached into his jacket and withdrew her passport. 'I'll be more than happy to arrange your immediate departure.' He met Erin's gaze, his eyes hard and cold as he watched her nervously finger the passport.

'I need Kazim's passport too,' she said shakily, sick fear swilling in her stomach.

'No.'

'What do you mean—*no*? Legally he's my son.'

'In England maybe. But we're not in England,' Zahir said, with a grim finality that set Erin's temper alight.

'You can't kidnap him. I'll go to the British Embassy,' she cried wildly. 'I agreed to bring him to Qubbah to visit your father, and I trusted that you would not stop me taking him back to Ingledean. You can't go back on your word.'

'I did not say anything about you taking Kazim away from Qubbah,' Zahir shrugged his shoulders impatiently, as if bored with the argument. '*You* are free to leave whenever you like. But *he* is staying here at the palace—for good.'

'No! You can't do that.'

Erin's face drained of colour, and Zahir felt the faintest tug on his conscience. Her eyes were huge in her pale face, and her vibrant hair seemed to have a life of its own, fighting free of the pins that secured it to tumble around her shoulders.

She was so beautiful, he thought angrily, infuriated by his body's unbidden response to her. He had never met a woman so exquisitely lovely, or wanted one with such shaming hunger. But the level of his desire for her surprised him. He had spent his adult life enjoying the company of beautiful women—women who were sophisticated and worldly and who played the game by his rules, and who did not have a criminal record for theft. So why did his libido go into overdrive whenever he looked at Erin?

She had been Faisal's wife—his *sister-in-law*, for pity's sake! He gave a bitter laugh and swung away from her as an unwelcome thought seeped into his mind. Did he want her *because* she had been married to Faisal? Was his feeling of satisfaction that she shared this wildfire sexual awareness more acute because he still had a score to settle with his dead brother? Faisal had stolen the woman he loved, and now he wanted to turn the tables? Or was he simply a man who had taken one look at a woman and been consumed by a desperate, overwhelming hunger to possess her, and nothing—not even the knowledge that she was an immoral gold-digger—could detract him from that need?

He glanced at her again, his eyes narrowing on the frantic rise and fall of her small breasts. She looked hot, and her thin skirt was clinging to her thighs. No doubt she wanted a shower after the long journey from England. To his self-disgust he pictured her stripping off her clothes and standing beneath the spray, smoothing soap over her flat stomach and then lower…

Heat surged through him and his nostrils flared. She was glaring up at him, clearly incandescent with rage that he had outwitted her, but the chemistry between them was so intense it was almost tangible, and the message in her stormy grey eyes was one he could not ignore.

'Of course you don't *have* to leave,' he murmured. 'I appreciate that Kazim is emotionally attached to you, and for his sake it might be better if you remained here—at least until he is settled.'

Erin shook her head so that her curls flew about her face. 'Wild horses couldn't drag me away from him,' she vowed fiercely. 'I will never, ever leave him.'

'In that case it looks as though we're stuck with each other—but there could be compensations for our enforced union,' he drawled, his voice suddenly soft and sensuous, sliding over her and sending a shiver of awareness the length of her spine.

Suddenly he was too close, although Erin hadn't been aware that he had moved. She could feel the heat of his body, and her senses quivered as she inhaled the exotic musk of his cologne. He was watching her with eyes that were suddenly hooded and slumberous, focusing intently on her mouth. She knew what he was thinking, but reacted seconds too late when he suddenly lowered his head towards her.

'Don't you dare touch me.' The words that had started out as an angry cry left her lips as a desperate plea that he ignored with supreme arrogance, claiming her mouth in a hard, possessive kiss that drove every logical thought from her mind and left nothing but her overwhelming awareness of him in its place.

His arms closed around her, caging her against his hard body, and she gave a shocked gasp, muffled beneath his mouth when she felt the rigid proof of his arousal nudge insistently between her thighs. She hated him, she reminded herself desperately. He was a cheat and a liar, and his threat to keep Kazim permanently at the palace was nothing short of diabolical. But the determined thrust of his tongue between her lips was a temptation she was pathetically powerless to resist, and she opened her mouth, allowing him access to her moist inner warmth. He slid his hand to her head and released the few remaining pins, and as her hair uncoiled in a sheet of rippling red silk down her back he made a low feral noise deep in his throat that sent an answering quiver of desire through her.

Every lesson she had learned about self-protection seemed to have deserted her. Nothing mattered except that she should assuage the clamouring need that started low in her pelvis and radiated out until every nerve ending was acutely sensitive to the feel of Zahir's hands and mouth on her skin. He released her lips, leaving them stinging and swollen, and trailed his mouth down her throat and along her collarbone, then lower still, his fingers deftly freeing the buttons of her blouse to reveal her small round breasts cupped by her lacy bra.

'Zahir!' She gave a startled cry when he suddenly lifted her, and the room whirled in a kaleidoscope of rich colours before he laid her on the bed and came down beside her, one heavy thigh anchoring her to the satin bedspread. This was dangerous, and she should stop him now, a voice in her head warned. But it was also new and exciting, and when he trailed his lips over the swell of her breast she shivered and held her breath—wanting more, wanting him to…

He eased her bra cup aside with long, tanned fingers that contrasted starkly with her pale flesh. She heard him mutter something in Arabic when he exposed her dusky pink nipple, and for a few seconds he stared down at her, his eyes glittering with a fierce hunger, before he lowered his head and stroked his tongue delicately over the rosy crest.

Sensation speared her and she whimpered with pleasure, sliding her hands to his shoulders and digging her nails into him in her desperation for him to continue. She felt weak and boneless, and when he drew her nipple fully into his mouth she arched her back, giving herself up to the new and exquisite delight of sexual desire flooding through her veins.

'Undress me.'

The command was a low growl that resonated through her, and when she lifted her heavy lids she saw that Zahir's sharp cheekbones were stained with dull colour, his face a taut mask of undisguised hunger. Once again the voice in her head advised caution, but her body had a will of its own. Her fingers fumbled with his shirt buttons until eventually the last one was freed, and she pushed the material aside and ran her hands over olive-gold skin that felt like satin beneath her fingertips, while the mass of black hairs that covered his chest tickled her palms.

She traced the ridges of his powerful abdominal muscles and felt his stomach contract, heard him growl something against her skin as he dragged her bra strap down her arm to expose her other breast. She gasped when he caught her swollen nipple between his lips and sucked—hard—causing a peculiar sensation to spiral down through her body from her breasts to her pelvis.

She could feel the flood of sticky wetness between her legs and twisted her hips restlessly. She was burning up, and when he grabbed the hem of her skirt, thrust it roughly up to her waist and slid his hand between her thighs, she quivered with anticipation, knowing that he was going to touch her where no man had ever touched her before, and ease the throbbing ache that consumed her whole body.

His mouth claimed hers once more in a deep, drugging kiss while his fingers brushed lightly over her knickers, stroking up and down but in no hurry to ease the strip of lace aside. It was torture at its most refined, Erin thought as she lifted her hips and rubbed against his hand in an agony of need that made her want to scream with frustration.

'Please…' Her voice sounded shockingly desperate, but she didn't care. She was drowning in the wondrous sensations he was arousing in her, and more than anything she had ever wanted in her life she longed for him to remove the rest of her clothes and possess her completely.

The sudden buzzing noise in her ear sounded like an angry wasp, but it was loud enough to impinge on her dream-like state. She opened her eyes at the same time as Zahir cursed savagely and rummaged in his jacket for his mobile phone.

He spoke in Arabic, his voice no longer like molten honey but clipped and harsh, and when he ended the call he stared down at her, the flame of desire that had made his eyes gleam now extinguished, leaving them cold and contemptuous as he trailed a path over her naked breasts.

Ice replaced the heat in Erin's veins, and with a low cry she sat up and dragged her bra into place with trembling fingers. A few moments ago she had writhed beneath him, her body driven by an intense sexual desire she had never experienced before. But now her passion had drained away, and she felt sick with humiliation and self-disgust as she recalled her wanton response to him.

How could she have allowed him to make love to her without offering the slightest resistance? She hated him for the way he had cynically manipulated her into bringing Kazim to Qubbah—how he had played on her sympathy for his sick father. Yet Zahir had only had to touch her, kiss her, and she had obediently rolled over and begged him to take her like a common slut.

Her behaviour proved that she was her mother's daughter, she acknowledged on a wave of shame. It had been no secret on the rough housing estate where she had spent the first years of her childhood that her mother worked the streets to pay for her drug habit, and it had frequently been whispered that Jeannie Maguire *enjoyed* her chosen career, and invited numerous lovers as well as clients back to the rundown flat that had been Erin's home. She had hated the men who'd knocked on the door at all hours of the day and night, and she remembered how she used to climb into the big old wardrobe in her bedroom to block out the strange noises coming from her mother's room.

Perhaps it was those early experiences that had left her feeling that sex was dirty and shameful? Certainly she had never felt the curiosity about sex that had consumed the other girls at school, and as an adult she had been relieved to realise that she had scant interest in men. But all that had changed when she had walked into the library at Ingledean and come face to face with the most stunningly gorgeous male she had ever laid eyes on. Zahir had blown her away, she thought dismally. He had triggered feelings she had hoped never to have and awakened her to a sexual desire that was now desperate to be appeased. But not with him, she told herself fiercely. Not with a man who clearly did not respect her.

'My father wishes to see me,' Zahir announced, his harsh voice shattering the silence and dispelling the lingering sensual haze that still hovered between them. He rolled off the bed, refastened his shirt and snatched up his jacket, frowning when he noted Erin's ashen face and the haunting vulnerability in her grey eyes.

There was nothing vulnerable about his brother's widow, he reminded himself cynically as he strode over to the door. Erin was no different from the countless other women he had met throughout his life—money-hungry, highly sexually experienced and calculating. His hunger for her—this primitive urge to throw her down on the bed, push up her skirt and sink himself into her—was an irritating inconvenience he could do without.

He knew he must fight his desire for her. Erin had been his brother's wife and was legally his nephew's stepmother. In his father's eyes that made her a member of the family, and the King would be deeply perturbed if he heard that he had visited Erin's bedroom when she had been unchaperoned. His behaviour constituted a serious breach of palace protocol and it could not happen again, he acknowledged as he stepped into the corridor and closed her door firmly behind him. Erin was out of bounds. And as it was now obvious that he was unable to keep his hands off her, he would have to avoid her until such time that he could dismiss her back to England.

# CHAPTER FOUR

SHE refused to stay here for another day, Erin vowed the following morning as she stood at the nursery window, blinking back angry tears. She would not allow Zahir to manipulate her and treat her as if she was worthless—particularly where Kazim was concerned.

She screwed up her eyes against the brilliant glare of the sun and scanned the palace gardens. But only the peacocks that lived in the grounds were strutting along the paths, and there was no sign of a man or a small boy.

She'd spent the previous night plagued by memories of her shameful response to Zahir, and worrying over his shocking statement that he would never let her take Kazim back to England. Eventually she'd fallen into a restless sleep, and consequently had woken late. The sun had already been streaming through the blinds when she'd hurried to the nursery where Bisma, the nanny Zahir had appointed, had explained that 'His Royal Highness' had taken 'Prince Kazim' for a camel ride in the desert.

How dared he take Kazim out without checking with her first? She was his legal parent and, like it or not, Zahir had to respect her role in his nephew's life. And how much longer were they going to be? she fretted anxiously. They had been gone for two hours. Surely Zahir would not have taken a three-year-old far into the desert? It must be easy to get lost amid the towering dunes, and what if Kazim suffered from sunstroke or became dehydrated?

The sound of voices drifted up from below, and relief washed over her when she saw Zahir striding along by the ornamental pool with Kazim balanced on his shoulders. Kazim's joyful laughter carried up to her window and she felt a pang of jealousy. She had devoted her life to him for three years, but how could she compete with the roomful of wonderful toys Zahir had provided and camel rides? How could she compete with a man who was Kazim's blood relative? Especially when that blood was royal—a discovery she was still reeling from. Rich was one thing, but how could she compete with royalty?

Her eyes followed them as they walked beneath her window. She despised herself for the way her heart-rate accelerated at the sight of Zahir. He looked relaxed this morning, almost boyish, and she felt a little twinge of longing that he would smile at her the way he was smiling at Kazim. His hair gleamed like raw silk in the sunlight, and even from a distance it was impossible to ignore the impact of his blatant virility. He was a man unlike any other she had ever met, and although she hated to admit it she was utterly fascinated by him.

Just then he looked up, and his eyes locked with hers, held for a heartbeat—until she jerked back from the window, embarrassed that he had caught her staring at him.

Moments later Kazim burst through the door. 'Erin, I rode on a camel, and I stroked him,' he told her, his face glowing with excitement as he rushed across the room into her waiting arms.

'How wonderful,' she murmured, lifting him up and rubbing her cheek against his silky curls. 'Did you wear a hat when you were out in the hot sun?' She glared at Zahir, who had followed Kazim into the room and now stood in front of her, his hands on his hips and his head thrown back, looking utterly devastating in lightweight cotton trousers and a white shirt that contrasted with his bronzed skin.

'He was well protected,' he informed her curtly. 'I am not so irresponsible that I would take him out without a hat.'

His casual dismissal of her concerns fired her temper. He was so arrogantly confident that he could do whatever he liked, but Kazim was *her* responsibility, and she needed to lay down some ground rules. 'In future I would like you to inform me before you take Kazim out,' she said stiffly. 'Perhaps I need to remind you that he is *my* son. Faisal entrusted him to *me*.'

Zahir's eyes narrowed at the criticism in her tone. 'So he did,' he agreed silkily. 'And I wonder what methods of persuasion you employed to entice him to marry you? Did you respond to him as eagerly as you responded to me when I kissed you? Faisal was a lonely widower, and I imagine he stood no chance against you—young, beautiful...' he gave a mocking laugh '...sympathetic—and indispensable to his motherless baby son. No wonder he couldn't resist you.'

'What you're implying is...disgusting,' Erin snapped, scarlet-cheeked. 'In no way did I set out to seduce Faisal. Our relationship wasn't like that—' She halted abruptly beneath Zahir's cool stare. There was no need for him to know that her marriage to his brother had been anything but a conventional one.

'What *was* it like, then?' Zahir taunted, wondering why he was pursuing the subject. He didn't want to know the intimate details of her relationship with his brother. The image in his head of Faisal making love to her, touching her, caressing her pale limbs, caused acid to burn in the pit of his stomach, and he despised himself. Faisal was dead, for pity's sake! How could he be jealous of him?

Erin shook her head so that her flame coloured curls danced on her shoulders—silky, sensuous. He wanted to touch her hair, bury his fingers in the fiery mass and then tilt her head so that he could claim her mouth in a searing kiss that would drive all thoughts of Faisal and her other previous lovers from her mind.

With considerable effort he tore his eyes from the temptation of her lush pink mouth and said coolly, 'My father has requested to see you and Kazim. I will come back in an hour to escort you to his private quarters.' He paused and studied her pale blue sundress. She was standing with her back to the window, and in the bright sunlight the outline of her body was clearly visible through the gauzy material, while the narrow straps revealed slim white shoulders. Somehow she managed to look innocently virginal and at the same time gut-wrenchingly sexy, and his mouth thinned as he fought the insidious hunger that had taken up permanent residence in his loins. 'You will need to change into something more suitable for an audience with the King,' he said harshly. 'In Qubbah it is not respectful for a woman to reveal so much bare flesh in public.'

Erin's face flamed. Admittedly her dress left her shoulders exposed, but the hem of the skirt fell to her knees, and to her mind it was perfectly respectable. Zahir made her feel like a tart, and mortification made her voice sharp. 'What do you suggest I wear? A sack that covers me from head to foot? Or do you expect me to dress in robes and a veil?' she snapped.

'My father is a liberal-minded man who would not expect

you to wear clothes that are not part of your culture,' Zahir said tersely. 'But out of respect for him *I* expect you to dress and act with a little decorum—and to restrain your insolent tongue.'

On that parting shot he strode out of the room and slammed the door behind him with such savagery that Erin was surprised great cracks did not appear in the palace walls.

'Why is Zahir cross?' Kazim turned his huge brown eyes on her and his bottom lip quivered.

'He's not cross with you, darling,' Erin quickly reassured him. 'He would never be angry with you, Kazim.'

'Zahir's my friend.' The toddler nodded and his grin reappeared. 'Is he your friend too, Erin?'

*Oh, hell!* 'Kind of,' she muttered. She needed to change the subject fast, and heaved a sigh of relief when Kazim wriggled out of her arms and raced over to his train set.

Erin was determined not to be overawed when she met the King, but her heart was thumping as she clutched Kazim's hand and followed Zahir along the rabbit warren of marble-floored corridors to His Majesty's private quarters.

She had been unable to disguise her shock when Zahir had swept into her sitting room an hour after their last confrontation, no longer wearing western clothes but dressed in traditional white Arab robes. He looked—spectacular. There was no other way to describe him. He was exotic and mysterious and supremely masculine, and she found herself fantasising about the muscular, olive-skinned body concealed beneath the thin cotton garment.

'I hope my outfit meets with your approval?' she hissed—aggression was her only defence against the feelings he aroused in her—when he halted outside the door of his father's sitting room, where two uniformed guards stood, holding fearsome-looking swords. Her white blouse had long sleeves and a high collar, and teamed with a plain navy blue skirt she could have passed for a Victorian governess. Surely he could not find fault now, when the only bit of her body on display was her ankles?

Zahir trailed his dark eyes over her in cool appraisal and pictured unfastening each of the tiny pearl buttons that ran down the front of her blouse slowly, one by one, revealing inch by inch her creamy skin and the firm swell of her breasts. Then he would remove the clasp that secured her hair in a knot on top of her head and spread her vibrant, silky curls over her shoulders, slide his hand to her nape and angle her mouth for his possession…

'You'll do,' he grated, as the guards stood aside to allow them to pass. 'Just remember to keep your mouth shut every time you're tempted to speak your mind, and hopefully you won't upset anyone.'

Erin gave him a saccharine smile and resisted the temptation to slap his haughty face. 'I'll do my best, My Lord.'

But her angry retort faded when she stared around the sumptuously decorated room. At the far end, sitting on a gold brocade sofa, was an elderly man, his grey hair and long silver beard just visible beneath his headdress.

Zahir had told her that his father was seriously ill, and too frail to travel to Ingledean, but King Kahlid stood up and walked towards them with surprising vigour. From the corner of her eye Erin saw Zahir bow, and she quickly dipped her head, but Kazim grinned at his grandfather.

'I went on a camel,' he told the King cheerfully. 'And I saw a pea-green falcon.'

'A green falcon?' King Kahlid looked confused.

'A peregrine falcon,' Zahir gently corrected his nephew, and the King chuckled and ruffled Kazim's hair.

'No formality today, Zahir,' he murmured, resting his hand briefly on his son's shoulder before he turned his gaze to Erin. 'And you must be Erin. I understand that you were married to my son Faisal and you are Kazim's adoptive mother?' He glanced down at Kazim—who had turned suddenly shy and was clinging tightly to her, with his face buried in her skirt—and added softly, 'I can see that Kazim is very fond of you.'

'As I am of him,' she replied fiercely. 'I love him as if he were my own child, Your Highness.'

The King's dark eyes seemed to look into her soul, as if he could read her innermost thoughts. The silence stretched Erin's nerves to breaking point, but then he smiled warmly and ushered her over to the sofa. 'Come and tell me all about him. You have cared for him since he was a few months old, I believe, so you must know him better than anyone…' his voice faltered '…now that my son is dead.'

Tears glistened in the elderly King's eyes and his voice was gruff when he spoke again. 'I will regret to the end of my days that I was not reconciled with my son before his death. Faisal spent his last years estranged from his family and in a foreign land, but I am comforted by the knowledge that he was not alone. He had you,' he said simply, smiling gently at Erin. 'Did you love my son, Erin?'

Taken aback by the question, Erin did not know how to answer. She could feel Zahir's dark eyes boring into her and knew what he was thinking—that she had callously married Faisal knowing that she would soon be a rich widow. It wasn't true, of course, and as she thought of the man she had married a year ago she suddenly relaxed and met the King's gaze.

'Yes, I loved him,' she said honestly. She had not been *in love* with Faisal, but he had been like a big brother to her. He'd been the only person apart from her foster parents who had been prepared to give her a chance and accept her for the woman she had become, rather than the unhappy and rebellious teenager she had once been.

She had met him fresh from the humiliation of being sacked from her first job as nanny to the Fitzroy children, and Faisal had believed her when she'd explained that, far from flirting with Giles Fitzroy, she had hated his revolting sexual innuendoes, and his suggestion that she could improve her career prospects by sleeping with him. When she'd finally found the courage to accuse the balding, middle-aged barrister of sexual harassment she'd been fired on the spot, and the furious Giles Fitzroy had insisted to his wife that it had been Erin who had wanted an affair. The story had quickly circulated among the Fitzroys' social group, and her chances of finding another job had seemed non-existent until Faisal had chosen her over several other applicants to care for his baby son, explaining that he believed Erin would give Kazim the love and attention he would have received from his mother.

'Faisal was a very special man,' she told the King softly.

King Kahlid nodded. 'And now you have been left alone to bring up his son. Some would say that that is quite a burden on such young shoulders. You have your whole life ahead of you, and although you loved Faisal, I'm sure you will not wish to be alone for ever. One day you may fall in love and even wish to marry again.'

What had Zahir been saying? Erin wondered furiously, recalling how he had accused her of planning to satisfy her sensual nature by taking lovers. Had he suggested to the King that she was an unsuitable mother for Kazim? She glanced across to where he was sitting, with the toddler on his knee, but his shuttered expression gave no clue to his thoughts. 'I have no plans to marry again, Your Highness,' she told the King steadily. 'When I adopted Kazim I vowed to devote my life to him, and that is exactly what I intend to do.'

King Kahlid nodded. 'I see that my son was very lucky to have found you,' he said gravely. 'And at least we, his family, can help you in your task now that you have brought Kazim to live here at the palace.'

'Oh, but I haven't—' Erin broke off, her heart plummeting. The King was beaming at Kazim, and he was clearly delighted when the little boy slid off Zahir's lap and trotted over to him.

'He fills my heart with joy,' the elderly monarch murmured in a choked voice. 'He is the image of his father, and God willing I will have a few years yet to watch him grow up.'

How could she break it to the King that she planned for Kazim to spend his childhood in England? Erin wondered frantically. It would break the old man's heart if she took the little boy away from the palace. She felt as though she had fallen into a trap from which there was no escape, and it was all Zahir's fault, she thought bitterly. He had tricked her into bringing Kazim to Qubbah, and now the King believed that his grandson was going to stay for ever.

Kazim had brought a toy fire engine from the nursery and, having grown bored with the conversation going on above his head, was now whizzing the vehicle across the marble floor and through the legs of the King's chair. His grandfather chuckled and turned to Zahir. 'He's a fine boy, isn't he, Zahir? A boy any man would be proud to call his son.'

'Indeed,' Zahir replied stiffly, forcing a smile that he hoped disguised his irritation from his father. Before he had left for England he'd spoken to the King of his intention to bring Kazim to Qubbah and raise him as his own child. He was more than willing to be a father to Faisal's son, and he already loved the little boy, but now there was an unexpected problem in the form of Faisal's second wife. It was customary under Qubbah's ancient traditions for a man to become the head of his dead brother's family and to marry his widow—but if his father believed there was any chance *that* was going to happen he had better think again!

'If you will excuse me, I have some work to attend to,' he said, bowing his head to the King. 'I believe Erin has brought some photographs to show you of Faisal, and of Kazim when he was a small baby. I've already seen them,' he added, in response to his father's querying gaze.

'Then go now. But I would like to see you later. There is something I wish to discuss with you,' the King said, in a genial tone that did not fool Zahir for a minute. He could always tell when his father was up to something. With a curt nod he strode from the room.

On the flight from England he had flicked through the album he'd found in Faisal's study, and his throat had ached with suppressed emotion at the pictures of his brother, whom he had not seen for six years. The photos recording Kazim's development were delightful, but there were other shots of Erin and Faisal, pictures that were clear evidence of a shared warmth between them he had not expected.

Could he possibly have misjudged her? Or was she simply

a talented actress who had been lying through her back teeth when she'd told his father she had loved Faisal? And why the hell did he feel as though he'd been kicked in the stomach at the idea that she really *had* married Faisal because she had been in love with him? Anger formed a tight knot in his chest—anger, and incomprehension of the violent jealousy that made him want to hit something.

He must look at it rationally, he told himself impatiently. Erin was a beautiful woman and he desired her. End of story. He had desired many women in his time, and without fail had persuaded them into his bed with an ease that had become almost boring. If Erin had been any other woman he would have wasted no time in bedding her—but, whatever her reasons for marrying Faisal, she was his widow and he could not seduce her.

Perhaps it was the knowledge that she was forbidden that made her even more alluring? Wasn't it human nature to desire most the thing you could not have?

Living under the same roof as her threatened to be purgatory, he acknowledged grimly, even taking into account the vastness of the palace. Even worse, he had promised his father that he would cut back on his trips abroad so that he could spend more time attending to matters of state. It would be many years before Kazim could rule Qubbah, and King Kahlid had already made it clear that on his death he expected Zahir to rule until Kazim came of age.

Zahir loved his homeland, but he was going to miss his freedom. He had always enjoyed spending time at his homes in London, St Tropez and New York, and up until recently he'd kept mistresses at all three locations. Out of respect to his father he'd always kept his affairs discreet, and he certainly

could not invite his lovers to the palace. But he had a healthy
sex drive, and he could see that it would not be long before
he was climbing the walls with frustration—a situation made
a hundred times worse when he was tormented by X-rated
fantasies about his sexy sister-in-law.

Erin spent the rest of the morning with the King, who was
plainly captivated by his little grandson and insisted—much
to the obvious concern of his manservant Aswan—on
crawling about on his hands and knees to play with him. For
his part Kazim seemed to have taken an instant liking to his
grandfather, but as Erin watched the two of them playing her
confusion increased.

   Zahir had told her that his father was seriously ill. Indeed,
he had insisted on rushing her and Kazim away from
Ingledean and given her the impression that the King was
close to death. But, although King Kahlid was old and
somewhat frail-looking, he was surprisingly sprightly and
appeared to be in good health.

   Zahir had treated her as if she was a puppet and he was
holding the strings, she thought angrily when she took Kazim
back to the nursery for his lunch.

   Her fears that she had been manipulated into a situation
from which there was no escape deepened further when Kazim
had settled for his nap and the nanny, Bisma, showed her a map
of the palace so that she could begin to find her way around.

   Despite the air-conditioning, she was so hot that her hair
was clinging in damp tendrils to her neck, and she desperately
needed to do something to relieve the tension that gripped her
muscles. 'I think I'll go and have a swim while Kazim is
asleep,' she said, indicating a nearby pool on the map.

'Oh, but you cannot swim in *that* pool,' Bisma informed her. 'It is overlooked by the palace windows and anyone could see you. You must swim in the pool in the women's quarters.'

'Women's quarters! I honestly think I've stepped back in time to another century,' Erin muttered. 'Next you'll be telling me I'm to join the harem.'

Bisma shook her head and explained seriously, 'King Kahlid's father was the last ruler to keep a harem. Since our beloved Royal Highness became King the men of Qubbah have mostly followed his lead and only take one wife.'

'Well, that's good to know,' Erin said sarcastically. But for some reason she found herself wondering who Zahir would marry. Would *he* only take one wife? She knew he was in his late thirties, but he did not seem in any hurry to marry one woman, let alone half a dozen. 'Why is Prince Zahir not married?' she asked Bisma curiously. 'I know that the King had arranged for Faisal to marry, and that he eloped with another man's fiancée. But why didn't King Kahlid choose a wife for his second son?'

'The King *did* choose Prince Zahir a bride, and the Prince fell in love with her—' Bisma broke off, a curious expression in her eyes when she stared at Erin.

For some inexplicable reason Erin felt a dull weight settle in her chest as she imagined Zahir in love with some unknown beauty—laughing with her, making love to her…Jealousy stabbed sharply in her heart, although she did not know why when she had convinced herself that she loathed him. She feigned uninterest when she queried, 'So why didn't they get married?'

Bisma looked uncomfortable, and she refused to meet Erin's gaze as she suddenly became absorbed in her task of folding the mountain of tee shirts that had been delivered for Kazim. 'I do not know. It was several years ago, and I have only heard gossip from my cousin, who works for the King's daughter, Princess Fatima.'

Erin nodded. She already knew that Zahir had three older sisters who were all married and had families of their own. But she was intrigued to hear more about Zahir's near-marriage experience.

Bisma was clearly worried that she had been indiscreet. 'It is not my place to talk of the Royal Family's personal affairs,' she mumbled, and would not be drawn further.

Erin sighed and wandered over to the window. The palace gardens were an exquisite oasis of green lawns and vibrantly colourful plants, but beyond the outer walls the desert stretched as far as the eye could see—a vast, arid landscape that was alien and frightening. The sight of it made her heart sink even further. She had lost all desire for a swim now that she knew she would be relegated to the 'women's quarters'. What kind of place was this? she thought dismally. She didn't belong here in this gilded prison, and nor did Kazim. She was sure Faisal had wanted him to grow up at Ingledean, and despite Zahir's insistence that he would remain at the palace she was determined to take him home.

'I have to speak to Zahir,' she announced tersely. She had already gleaned from Bisma that Zahir's private quarters were on the opposite side of the palace, but when she marched towards the door, her face set, the nanny glanced up in alarm.

'You cannot go to the Prince's quarters alone and uninvited,' she said anxiously, staring at Erin as though she feared Zahir would have her thrown into the ancient fortress's dungeons if she dared to disturb him.

But Erin's mind was made up. 'Watch me,' she told Bisma coolly, and, mentally preparing herself for battle, she swept out of the nursery.

It would be easy to disappear without trace in the miles of corridors that wound through the vast palace, she decided some twenty minutes later, when she finally negotiated her way to the east wing.

'Will I find Prince Zahir here?' she asked the hapless guard who had followed her from her side of the palace, and who had looked increasingly unhappy when she had steadfastly refused to return to her suite.

He did not reply, but she saw him exchange glances with the two guards standing at the end of the corridor. She was certain she would find Zahir beyond the double doors.

'I'm here to see the Prince,' she told them, lifting her chin and glaring at them when they stared straight ahead, their faces impassive. 'He is expecting me.' The lie still earned no response, and with an angry toss of her head she stepped forward—only to find her way instantly barred as the guards crossed their swords in front of the doors.

'It is not permitted for you to enter.' One of the men finally spoke, and Erin's brows shot up.

'Oh, so you *can* understand me? Well, understand this: I wish to see His Highness, and I intend to see him right now.'

'You cannot.'

As she put her hand on the door one of the guards caught hold of her arm, his eyes gleaming as he said something in Arabic to his companion that Erin was certain from his tone and the derogatory sneer on his face was not a compliment. A red mist of rage swirled in front of her eyes as she struggled free of his grasp. Her temper had been smouldering like a sleeping volcano since she had arrived in Qubbah, and now it erupted in a cataclysmic explosion.

'Take your hands off me.' She spun around, intending to hammer her fist against the door and gain Zahir's attention, but somehow amidst the confusion she caught the guard squarely on the nose, and he let out a startled howl that echoed along the corridor.

*'What is going on...?'* The doors were suddenly flung open and Zahir appeared, his brows drawn into a thunderous frown as he surveyed Erin surrounded by three angry guards, one of whom was trying to stem the blood pouring from his nose.

'I'm so sorry—I didn't mean it—it was an accident,' Erin gasped, her gaze swinging frantically from the injured guard to Zahir, who was towering over her, the look of stunned disbelief in his eyes turning to one of savage fury. She peered past him into what appeared to be a boardroom, and paled at the sight of six men wearing traditional Arab robes, who had got to their feet and were now staring at her, patently dumbstruck that she'd had the audacity to barge in on the Prince. 'I need to talk to you,' she mumbled, her spurt of defiance trickling away and leaving her wishing she could sink into the floor.

'That much is obvious,' Zahir said coldly. 'I was in the middle of discussing important matters of state, but don't let that worry you. I'm sure that whatever you want to say is far more urgent than the drought which is causing such hardship to the people of Qubbah,' he added sarcastically.

'I'll come back later,' Erin whispered, her cheeks flaming with embarrassment. Zahir looked as though he could cheerfully strangle her, and innate honesty forced her to admit that she couldn't blame him.

Zahir's hand shot out and gripped her arm, preventing her hurried retreat. 'Oh, no,' he growled, 'after the disruption you've caused, you're not going anywhere.'

He turned his head and spoke briefly in Arabic to the men grouped around the boardroom table, then barked instructions to the still bleeding guard, presumably ordering him to seek medical attention, before he frogmarched Erin across the corridor and through another set of doors into what she guessed was his private office.

Her heart sank still further when Zahir's personal assistant, Omran, leapt to his feet, a look of avid interest on his face when he glanced at her and then at his master's thunderous expression.

'Your Highness, I had not expected your meeting with the committee to finish so soon.'

'The meeting isn't finished—merely postponed,' Zahir informed him through gritted teeth. He did not look at Omran but continued to glare furiously at Erin. 'We were interrupted by unforeseen circumstances,' he added harshly.

His assistant looked as though he was about to explode with curiosity, but protocol prevented him from asking further questions and he murmured, 'Do you wish me to escort Erin back to her quarters, Your Highness?'

'No, I wish you to make my apologies to the committee and arrange a date for another meeting. I will deal with Erin,' Zahir said, in a tone that sent a trickle of ice down Erin's spine.

She had never seen him so angry, and she knew that the most sensible thing to do would be to apologise for disturbing him. But why should *she* be the one to apologise? He had brought her here under false pretences, and she had every right to demand that he put her and Kazim on the next flight back to England.

Her new spurt of defiance wavered slightly when Omran reluctantly sidled out of the office and closed the door behind him, leaving her alone with a grim-faced Zahir, who suddenly released his hold on her so that she stumbled and fell onto a silk-covered chaise longue. He prowled around his desk like a caged tiger before coming to a halt directly in front of her.

'I can't believe you attacked a palace guard, you crazy wildcat. What the hell was all that about?' he demanded coldly, his jaw tightening ominously when Erin lifted her chin and met his gaze with a boldness she did not feel.

'I came to tell you that I'm going home,' she snapped, 'and to demand that you hand over Kazim's passport, because I'm taking him with me.'

Black eyebrows winged upwards, and he stared down his nose at her with such disdainful hauteur that her fingers itched to slap him. He was an arrogant pig—but unfortunately he looked like a golden-skinned demi-god in black tailored trousers and a white silk shirt which was so fine that she could clearly make out the ridges of his powerful abdominal muscles beneath it.

She felt a peculiar squirmy feeling low in her stomach, and her breasts suddenly felt full and heavy as she remembered what had happened after she had angered him when they had first arrived at the palace. He had kissed her as a means of punishing her, and his mouth had been hard and dominant as he'd sought to subjugate her. But somehow passion had slowly taken the place of his fury, and he had traced his hands and lips over her body as if he could not resist the temptation of her delicately perfumed skin. He had aroused her to a fever pitch of desire, and the memory of how he had caressed her with his hands and mouth was a permanent fixture in her brain.

Frantically she dragged her mind from her wanton thoughts. Her face felt hot, and his narrow-eyed glance warned her that he was well aware of the effect he had on her.

'We've been through this before,' he drawled in a bored tone. 'And I have told you that you are free to leave at any time you wish. But Kazim will remain here in Qubbah. It is his rightful place, homeland of his forefathers and his heritage,' he added coolly, in a tone that warned he did not expect her to argue further.

'And he is heir to the throne—a little fact that you forgot to mention at Ingledean, when you persuaded me to bring him here,' she said icily. 'I suppose you were too busy making up all that rubbish about your father being on his deathbed—so ill that he could not possibly fly to England to visit his grandson. You lied to me.' She rounded on him bitterly. 'You led me to believe that the King might only have a short time left and that he was desperate to see Kazim before he died. But your father is no nearer to death than I am,' she snapped. 'For a man of eighty he looks as fit as a flea.'

Burning up with anger because Zahir had manipulated her into doing his bidding, she missed the warning glint in his eyes. 'You tricked me into bringing Kazim here, but you are not keeping him. It was his father's wish that he should spend his childhood at Ingledean with me. I know what Faisal wanted,' she flung at him, pushing her tumbling flame-coloured curls over her shoulder with an impatient flick of her hand.

Zahir's body clenched in rejection of her last statement and he felt the same, humiliating jealousy that always gripped him whenever he though of Erin with his brother. *I know what Faisal wanted.* She had been referring to Faisal's wishes for Kazim's upbringing after his death, but the words swirled in his head, taunting him. Had she learned what Faisal wanted in bed and enjoyed pleasing him? Or had she cleverly pandered to his desires as part of her plan to persuade him to marry her, knowing that her willingness between the sheets would one day earn her ownership of Ingledean House?

He wanted her gone, he thought darkly—out of the palace, out of Qubbah, and out of his head. He hated the hold she had on his hormones—hated the fact that, despite wanting her more desperately than he had ever wanted a woman in his life, he could not make love to his dead brother's wife. It was bad enough that he had kissed her when she had angered him yesterday. If he had not been interrupted by Omran's phone call had he was ashamed to admit that he would not have been able to pull back. He would have taken her with all the finesse of a callow boy, he acknowledged grimly. For reasons that were beyond him Erin had a devastating effect on his self-control, and he despised himself for his weakness.

'If you allow me to take Kazim back to Ingledean, I promise I will bring him back to Qubbah for regular visits,' Erin said in a quieter tone. 'You deliberately deceived me about your father's state of health, and if you continue to prevent me from taking Kazim I will appeal to the King. I can't believe he asked you to lie about him. *He* is an honourable man, and I'm sure he would not stoop to "playing dirty",' she added, recalling Zahir's unashamed confession that he would go to any lengths to get his own way.

Zahir felt his anger ignite at her implication that she believed his father to be honourable but that he, Prince Zahir bin Kahlid al Muntassir, lacked that most valued virtue. 'I suggest that you keep away from my father—unless you want to suffer the full force of my anger,' he growled furiously.

'Despite what you think, the King is no longer physically strong. He hates anyone to know it, and has only allowed me to take on some of the workload of running the kingdom after considerable persuasion. I will not allow him to be troubled by a hot-tempered, violent gold-digger,' he continued in that same hard voice, ignoring Erin's outraged gasp. 'At Ingledean I offered you a considerable sum of money to give up Kazim.'

'Money that I refused,' Erin said sharply. 'I agreed to bring him myself, in good faith, believing that it was only for a short visit.'

'But Kazim is happy here, and you cannot deny that. If you return to England alone and sign over full custody of him to me I will treble the offer I made to you.'

Nausea surged in Erin's stomach, and her face twisted as she swallowed the bile in her throat. How could she possibly be so attracted to this man? It was said that the eyes were the mirrors of the soul, and Zahir's eyes were cold and so pitiless that she shivered.

'You don't get it, do you?' she grated, her throat feeling as if someone had taken a piece of sandpaper to it. 'I wouldn't part with Kazim if you offered me the moon and the stars and the whole world. Kazim is my son. You can keep your filthy money—he is not for sale!' She jumped to her feet, breathing hard at his assessment of her character as a hot-tempered, violent gold-digger. Oh, she was hot-tempered, all right—and as for violent! Acting on impulse, she snatched up the heavy paperweight on his desk and flung it at him. 'I hate you—do you hear me?' And she hated herself more, for her humiliating fixation with him.

Her anger intensified when he caught the paperweight with insulting ease and set it carefully back down on the desk. 'I honestly think you could be insane. You're certainly unbalanced,' he hissed, his eyes flashing fire as he closed in on her. 'As for hating me…' His laugh grated on her raw nerves and his mouth curved into a cynical smile as he watched her step back until her legs hit the edge of the chaise longue and she realised she had no way of escaping him. 'Our mutual dislike of each other is not in dispute, Erin—but neither is the sexual hunger that torments us both. I know from the dark shadows beneath your eyes that you didn't sleep last night, and I know what kept you awake—because I too tossed and turned between the sheets and fantasised about doing this…'

## CHAPTER FIVE

ZAHIR'S dark head swooped and his mouth sought hers with unerring precision. His tongue skilfully traced the contours of her lips, but she twisted her head and braced her hands against his chest, despair sweeping through her when her senses reacted to the sensual heat of his body and the subtle musk of his cologne. She could not let him kiss her—not again, no way, never!

'You're mistaken,' she muttered. 'I don't feel anything for you—and the only reason I didn't sleep last night is because I'm desperate to take Kazim and leave here.'

'Liar,' Zahir drawled lazily. One hand cupped her chin and forced her head up while the other anchored in her hair to hold her fast. 'You assure me you want to leave, but your body tells a different story.' He trailed his eyes down her body to the visible peaks of her nipples straining beneath her blouse and gave a satisfied smile.

She looked so prim and proper in the high-necked blouse and long skirt she'd worn for her meeting with the King, but her demure appearance only inflamed his hunger for her. He knew damn well that her air of innocence was an illusion, and he preferred his lovers to be confident and experienced rather than timid virgins, but when she blushed and stared at him with her huge, faintly stunned grey eyes he felt a primitive need to claim her as *his* woman and his alone, to make love to her with such fierce passion that she acknowledged him as her master.

'I know what you want, Erin.' His voice had thickened and his warm breath fanned her earlobe, sending a shiver of delicious sensation down Erin's spine. 'You want me to strip the clothes from your body, spread you beneath me and take you hard and fast, drive us both to the edge of reason and the very heights of sexual ecstasy.'

'No!' She valiantly tried to shut her ears to his seductive voice, to shut her mind to the stark images in her head that his whispered words evoked. His fingers tightened on her chin, forcing her head round so that he could claim her mouth, and with a strength born of desperation she kicked him hard on the shin. 'I'd rather go to bed with a rattlesnake than with you.'

He swore savagely and loosened his grip—but only momentarily. 'You vicious little vixen—it's time you were tamed,' he growled, catching her around the waist when she tried to dart past him, and pushing her down onto the chaise longue. He immediately covered her body with his own, his weight pinning her to the cushions, and the feel of his rock-hard erection jabbing into her belly caused liquid fire to pool between her thighs.

'Let me up, you barbarian.' She beat her fists on his shoulders until he captured her wrists in one of his big hands and forced her arms above her head so that she could inflict no further damage.

'If my father knew what a wildcat you are, I'm sure he would not be so eager for me to marry you,' Zahir muttered grimly.

The shocked silence that followed his astounding statement was shattered by the sound of Erin's hysterical laughter. 'Your father wants *us* to *marry*? And you say *I'm* insane? Why on earth would he make such a ridiculous suggestion?' she demanded, refusing to be cowed when he glared down at her, his eyes glittering with anger.

'For Kazim's sake, of course—what other reason could there be?' Zahir's jaw hardened when he recalled his lunchtime conversation with his father, during which the King had referred to Erin's statement that she had no plans to marry again. She'd vowed to devote herself to Kazim, and as Zahir had pledged to be a father to the little boy a marriage of convenience between him and his brother's beautiful young widow seemed highly sensible—and indeed his duty.

Besides, it was time he settled down, King Kahlid had pressed, when Zahir had muttered something along the lines of 'over my dead body'. He was thirty-six, and in a few years from now, perhaps less, would be the interim ruler of Qubbah. He needed a wife—and who better for him to marry than the mother of the future heir of the kingdom?

Nothing would sway the King from his belief that marriage between his remaining son and his dead son's widow was an excellent plan, and Zahir's hints that Erin might not be quite as saintly as she appeared had brought only a heavy frown from his father.

'I am convinced that her love for the boy is genuine, and that is all that matters,' King Kahlid had stated, with a finality that had ended further argument.

For a second Zahir had been tempted to reveal the facts his personal assistant had discovered about Erin's past, but he had kept quiet. His father was old and frail, and it was clear he wanted to believe she had made Faisal happy in the last months of his life. But Zahir did not share the King's belief that she was all sweetness and light, and as he stared down at her flushed face, and the lush mouth that would tempt a saint, he gave a harsh laugh.

'You are the last woman I would choose to be my wife, I assure you. But my father is anxious for Kazim to have a stable upbringing, with two parents who will take the place of his own.'

Of course it was for Kazim's sake, Erin acknowledged, her heart beating so fast that she could barely breathe. And she knew why King Kahlid might have made such an outrageous proposal—if she married Zahir he could adopt Kazim and she would never be able to take him back to England. She would be stuck here for ever, trapped in a marriage made in hell, with no possible means of escape unless she left Kazim behind.

'Trust me, you're not my Mr Perfect either,' she snapped. 'But we can both breathe easy, because I wouldn't marry you if you were the last man on the planet.'

'Is that so? Lucky I have no wish to marry you, then,' Zahir said silkily. 'I just want to bed you.'

'How dare you?' His deliberate crudity fuelled her temper, but at the same time she felt a curious pain in her chest, as if he had stabbed her through the heart.

Before she could demand that he go to hell, he bent his head and brought his mouth down on hers in a statement of absolute possession, his tongue thrusting between her lips as if he was determined to prove his dominance over her. Erin tried to clamp her lips together, desperate to resist his mastery, but the need to fight him was being superseded by another, more primitive need—a hunger that only this man could arouse and only he could appease.

'Zahir—please!' When he finally broke the kiss she dragged oxygen into her lungs and made one last feeble plea, knowing that if he kissed her again she would be lost.

'Oh, I will please you, Erin,' he said softly, but it sounded like a threat rather than a promise, and she twisted her head wildly and bucked her hips—until she realised that her actions were having a profound effect on his already aroused body. 'Don't stop,' he mocked, when she ceased the frantic movements that had brought her pelvis into direct contact with the solid ridge of his throbbing manhood. 'But you're wearing too many clothes.'

With deft movements that proclaimed his expertise in the art of undressing a woman he one-handedly unfastened the row of tiny buttons that ran from Erin's throat to her waist, and pushed the edges of her blouse apart to reveal small breasts cupped by a gossamer-fine bra. Her nipples were clearly visible beneath the sheer fabric and he brushed his thumb-pad delicately across one peak and then the other, until she was desperate for him to caress her naked flesh.

His gaze locked with hers as he unhooked the clasp at the front of her bra and bared her breasts. With her wrists still pinned above her head, she was totally exposed to his hungry gaze, and a tremor of excitement ran through her when she saw the blaze of feral hunger in his eyes. 'This is what you like, Erin,' he taunted, his voice husky with sexual promise, and he flicked his tongue across one dusky pink crest.

The sensation was so exquisite that she gave a moan, half-pleasure half-shame. She couldn't fight him any longer, and when he drew the tight peak fully into his mouth she arched her back, her doubts and inhibitions swept away on a tidal wave of bliss.

Her innocent body recognised its tutor, and a quiver of longing racked her when he moved his mouth to her other breast, his wicked tongue lashing her nipple, stroking back and forth, until she sobbed his name and he relented, closing his lips fully around her aureole and sucking its sensitive tip. He must have sensed her total capitulation, because he released her wrists and she immediately curled her hands around his neck, burying her fingers in the silky hair at his nape.

Now both his hands were free to explore her, and he muttered something beneath his breath as he dragged her skirt up so that it bunched around her waist—and discovered that her sheer hose were in fact stockings, edged with a wide band of lace that held them in place around her slender thighs.

Thank the Almighty he hadn't known she was wearing *stockings* during their audience with the King—he doubted he'd have been able to keep his hands off her! But now he did not have to, and a bolt of white-hot need ripped through him as he slid his hand up one silk-covered leg until he reached the satiny strip of bare flesh revealed above the lace stocking-top. He felt the tremor that ran through her, heard her soft gasp when he moved his hand higher still, and his gut clenched as he eased his fingers beneath the edge of her knickers and stroked, gently but insistently, against her tightly closed lips.

Slowly, tentatively, she opened for him, and Zahir's breath hitched in his throat as he probed her sticky wet heat, slid deeper and felt her muscles contract around his fingers. She was unexpectedly tight, and he frowned as he felt the burgeoning length of his arousal quiver with impatient need. He wanted to strip her and spread her beneath him, ready for his possession, but Erin had tensed, her eyes tightly closed and her lush mouth slightly parted. He could feel her frantic little jerks against his hand, inciting him to increase the intimacy of his caresses, and he pushed deeper into her velvet folds, realising with a jolt of shock that she was about to climax. He quickened the pace of his fingers while he rubbed his thumb-pad delicately over her clitoris.

The effect was explosive, and Erin gave a sharp cry, her body as taut and arched as an overstrung bow, her fingers clawing at Zahir's shoulders as she surrendered to the tidal wave of pleasure that ripped through her. She was ready for him—and he couldn't wait, Zahir acknowledged, excitement and an urgent need to bury his shaft deep inside her eager body making his fingers clumsy as he fumbled with the zip of his trousers. He had lost all sense of time and place—driven by a primitive urgency for sexual release…

'Your Highness…forgive me…I did not realise…'

The sound of Omran's shocked voice smashed through the sexual haze that fogged Zahir's brain. Slowly he lifted his head and stared across the room, his chest heaving as he fought for control. He spoke in Arabic, barked a furious command to his personal assistant to get out, but the interruption had brought him to his senses, and he stared down at Erin, his face twisting with self-disgust.

What spell had she cast over him that had caused him to abandon his dignity and self-respect—let alone the respect of his staff—and had seen him behave like a rutting dog in the gutter?

Erin had blanched at the sound of Omran's voice, and her grey eyes were no longer smoky with passion but huge with shock. The faint shimmer of her tears filled Zahir with a mixture of guilt and fury. She had been with him all the way, he reminded himself. But now she looked young and gut-wrenchingly vulnerable, her vibrant red curls contrasting starkly with her paper-white face.

He had to get away from her before he gave in to the fire still coursing through his veins and pushed her back down onto the cushions. Despite his scalding embarrassment that his personal assistant had caught him in such a compromising situation, his urgency to possess Erin had not faded. But with a jerky movement he leapt to his feet and stared down at her, every muscle in his body clenching with sexual frustration.

'Cover yourself,' he growled, looking away from her while she dragged her blouse over her breasts with trembling fingers. 'The answer to your request to take Kazim to England is a resounding no,' he ground out harshly. 'His place is here. But yours is not. I suggest that for both our sakes you go back to the house on the moors that you worked so hard to acquire.'

He swung away from her, his conscience prickling as he thought of Kazim. The little boy loved Erin and regarded her as his mother. Would it be fair to separate him from the woman who had cared for him since he was a couple of months old? Zahir thought back to when his own mother had left Qubbah, to how desperately he had missed her and longed for her to return, and his heartbreak when he learned that she was never coming back. How could he allow Kazim to suffer the same sense of abandonment that had haunted what had remained of his childhood after his mother had gone?

But Kazim was younger than he had been, he reassured himself. He would soon forget Erin. He would have to, Zahir decided. Because the alternative was for her to remain at the palace indefinitely, and his hormones would go into meltdown.

He strode over to the door, but could not resist looking back at her. His desire for her had escalated to an agonising craving that was beyond anything he had ever felt for any other woman. She was forbidden to him while she remained Faisal's widow—but if she was his wife he would have exclusive rights to her exquisite body.

Marrying her would solve a number of problems—not least his unbearable sexual frustration, he acknowledged grimly as he turned his back on her and slammed out of the room. But was he really prepared to sacrifice his freedom and marry a woman he had good evidence was a gold-digger simply because he was desperate to take her to bed?

Erin scrambled to her feet and stared after Zahir's retreating form. Reaction was setting in: her legs were shaking and she felt sick with humiliation. She didn't know what was worse— being caught making love with Zahir by his personal assistant, or the look of utter contempt in Zahir's eyes when he had stared down at her half-naked body, spread before him like a concubine awaiting her master.

She couldn't stay here for another day, another hour, she thought wildly, burying her face in her hands in an effort to blot out the images of Zahir's hands on her body. The memory of his intimate caresses made her cheeks flame. Her first ever orgasm had been mind-blowing, but she shuddered when she recalled how she had sobbed and writhed in his arms. She would rather die than have to face him again.

'I have to get away from here,' she muttered to the empty room, and then gave a startled cry when a voice from behind her replied.

'I think that would be a most wise course of action,' Omran

murmured, stepping into Zahir's office and closing the door behind him. As usual he was excruciatingly polite, but behind his deferential smile Erin caught an insolent gleam in his eyes, and she blushed when his knowing gaze slid over her dishevelled hair and swollen mouth. 'His Highness Prince Zahir's interest in you is merely a temporary aberration,' he continued silkily. 'You can never be more than his mistress. One day he will marry a highborn Arab bride, and then your position here at the palace will be untenable. It is perhaps better if you leave now.'

Erin gave a tight smile. 'You really know how to make a girl feel good about herself, Omran,' she muttered sarcastically.

Zahir's personal assistant was almost as high and mighty as his employer—and that was saying something. She was tempted to tell him of the King's suggestion, that Zahir should marry her, just to wipe the smug smile off his face. But what was the point? she thought dispiritedly. Omran clearly believed she was less worthy of his royal master's attention than a pile of camel dung—a belief no doubt shared by Zahir himself.

'How can I leave?' she queried miserably. 'The palace guards tail my every move.' She broke off, thinking of the guard she had accidentally punched on the nose. It had not been the most edifying moment of her life, and it was small wonder that Zahir had accused her of being unbalanced. He was a royal prince, born into unimaginable wealth, and he could have no comprehension of her deprived childhood, during which she'd learned early on to fight to survive.

'The guards are under orders to protect young Prince Kazim. They have no interest in you if he is not with you,' Omran told her bluntly. 'The road from the palace leads across the desert to the capital, Al Razir. There is a fleet of four-by-fours parked in the courtyard in front of the staff quarters.'

Startled, Erin stared at him, her heart thumping. Omran was offering her a chance to escape—but he did not realise that she would never leave Kazim behind. 'Where would I find the keys to one of those cars?' she whispered.

In reply Omran walked over to Zahir's desk, pulled open a drawer and calmly took out a set of keys. 'This conversation never took place,' he murmured as he dropped them into her hand, and before Erin could utter another word he had turned—his long robes billowing behind him—and swept from the room as silently as a snake in the grass.

A few hours later Erin glanced in the rearview mirror of the four-by-four, hardly able to believe that she was not being chased across the desert by palace guards. She was amazed that her plan to smuggle Kazim out of the palace had worked so well, but guessed that Omran had had something to do with the absence of the guards who usually patrolled the fortress gates.

She had done it—she was free. All she had to do now was somehow locate the British Embassy and beg them to send her and Kazim home.

'Where we going, Erin?' Kazim's voice piped up from the rear seat.

'We're driving to the town, and maybe later we'll go on an aeroplane again. Would you like that?'

The toddler nodded his head vigorously, and she was assailed by guilt. He was so trusting—an innocent pawn caught up in a battle between two people who loved him— and, much as she despised Zahir, she had to admit that he seemed to adore the little boy almost as much as she did. She knew too that Kazim hero-worshiped his uncle. How was she going to explain to him that Zahir was not coming back to England with them? Was she really acting in his best interests—or her own?

Soon the walls of the fortress were no longer visible, and the desert seemed vast and intimidating. The sun was sinking below the horizon, and the streaks of gold and red that stained the sky were fading to purple as night fell with surprising swiftness. Erin's palms were clammy as she gripped the steering wheel. She switched on the headlights and stared intently through the windscreen. Omran had said that Al Razir was ahead, but he hadn't mentioned that the road forked, and she had no idea which way to go. It had to be straight on, she reasoned. She had no recollection of turning from one dusty track to another on the way to the palace, but if she was honest the journey to Zahir's home had been an endless blur of sand.

After driving for another half an hour it became obvious that she had taken the wrong road. The lights of Al Razir should surely be visible by now, but instead the blackness was thick and oppressive, and the road had changed from a reasonably flat surface to a narrowing track which twisted tortuously between boulders that loomed out of the dark. She was lost, and the only thing to do was turn around and go back to the fork where the road had separated, Erin decided, fighting her feeling of panic.

She braked and selected reverse gear, but as she turned the steering wheel she heard a sickening crunch of metal against something hard, and when she accelerated forward the car did not move.

'Wait there,' she ordered Kazim, trying to keep the tension

from her voice as she opened the door and jumped out onto the sand. A hurried inspection revealed that one of the back wheels had become tightly wedged between two rocks; the metal rim was buckled, and even if she could free it, it was clear that the vehicle would be undriveable. She was trapped in the vast, dark desert where the temperature had already plummeted.

She saw Kazim shiver, and knew in that moment that she had made the biggest mistake of her life. What had she been thinking of? The desert was an alien environment to her, and she must have been crazy to have risked driving across it alone. She had put Kazim's life at risk, and now she felt sick with fear and guilt. Zahir had said he thought she was insane, and right now she could offer no defence against his accusation.

'Erin, I want to go back now.'

Kazim sounded tired and Erin hastened to reassure him. 'We will, soon,' she said soothingly as she opened the rear door and wrapped her jacket around him.

'Zahir and me are going to play trains when we get home.'

'That'll be great.' She smiled at the little boy, anxious to hide her fear from him. She certainly couldn't reveal that she had no idea how they were ever going to get back to the palace.

Soon Kazim's breathing slowed and he fell asleep. Erin curled her arm around him and stared at the twin beams of light that shone from the headlights. She knew she risked flattening the car battery by leaving them on, but she couldn't bear sitting in the pitch-black. There was nothing she could do until daylight, but as time slipped slowly by she acknowledged that Zahir must have discovered by now that she had gone, and he would be desperately worried about Kazim.

Something suddenly caught her attention. She screwed up her eyes and peered into the night, her heart leaping when she realised that the lights in the distance were not a figment of her imagination. They were coming closer, and soon it was clear that they belonged to vehicles which were speeding across the desert; she could make out three sets of headlights and she felt weak with relief. Zahir must have organised a search party. But mixed with her joy at being found was trepidation. He was going to be *furious* with her—and she deserved every bit of his anger.

Minutes later the four-by-fours halted, and Zahir sprang from the lead vehicle. His expression was unfathomable as Erin quickly alighted from her car, but she caught the blaze of molten fury in his eyes and shrank back while he reached inside and lifted a still-sleeping Kazim into his arms. Members of the palace guard grouped around her, dark and unsmiling, and Zahir spoke to them in Arabic before he placed the toddler in the back of the second four-by-four, where the nanny was waiting.

Erin briefly caught sight of Bisma's anxious face, but the young Arab girl looked away from her. The guards climbed into the rear two cars and within seconds they were racing back across the desert with Kazim—leaving Erin alone with Zahir.

'Get in.' He held open the door of his four-by-four and she quickly complied. He had every right to lose his temper, even shout at her, she reminded herself, but he remained ominously quiet when he slid into the driver's seat, and when she dared risk a glance at him her heart lurched. Even now, when he looked as though he could happily commit murder, he still had a devastating effect on her. Dressed in black jeans and matching sweater, he was dark and dangerous but undeniably the sexiest man she had ever laid eyes on, and she simply could not control her reaction to him.

The silence shredded her nerves, and she was relieved when he started the engine. 'I'm sorry about damaging the car,' she muttered when it became clear that he intended to ignore her for the journey back to the palace. 'I realised I'd taken the wrong road to Al Razir and I was trying to turn round.' She paused, and then added in a low voice, 'I don't suppose you'll believe me, but I was going to bring Kazim back to the palace.'

Zahir said nothing, and with a heavy sigh she gave up. In the far distance she could see the red tail-lights of the other two cars, but when they reached the fork in the road Zahir turned away from them and sped off in the opposite direction.

Confused, Erin felt a frisson of unease. 'Where are we going? The palace is behind us, isn't it?'

Zahir finally deigned to acknowledge her presence and speared her with a brief, hard glance before looking away, as if the sight of her sickened him. 'I'm taking you to Al Razir,' he said, in a cold voice that froze Erin's blood. 'From there you will be escorted to the airport. You are booked onto a flight to England.'

Sheer panic churned in Erin's stomach. 'But what about Kazim?' she whispered.

'He is being driven back to the palace,' Zahir told her, still in that icy tone. 'As I have explained, many times, it is his home now.' His tenuous hold on his self-control gave way and his anger exploded. 'I can't believe you drove off into the desert with him. Your behaviour was stupid and irresponsible. The guards who had been assigned to watch over Kazim have been sacked for their incompetence,' he added, his voice shaking with fury.

'It wasn't their fault,' Erin said miserably. 'Your personal assistant is the one to blame. He helped me to get away, and even told me where I would find a car.'

'Don't be ridiculous—why do you imagine I would listen to your lies?' Zahir rounded on her furiously. 'Omran told me how he had caught you rifling through my desk, and he was deeply apologetic that he had not guessed you had stolen the car keys.'

'I did not steal them—he gave them to me—' Erin broke off, hurt mingling with anger at the look of scathing contempt in Zahir's eyes. It was clear that he had absolute faith in his personal assistant. 'Omran is sneaky and two-faced, and if you want my advice you should keep a close eye on him.'

'Fortunately I do not have to listen to your advice—indeed, with luck I will never have to see you again once you are back in England,' Zahir snapped.

'I won't go without Kazim,' Erin cried wildly. 'I've told you I will never leave him.' In desperation she caught hold of Zahir's arm, so that the car swerved, and he swore savagely and braked. Tears poured down her face as she fumbled with the door catch. 'I won't be separated from him, do you hear? I'll walk back to the palace if I have to.'

The sand was a reasonably forgiving surface when she jumped from the moving car, but it was hard enough, and she lay where she had landed, winded and struggling to breathe. Zahir had stopped the four-by-four a little way ahead and was already running back to her, shouting furiously in a mixture of English and Arabic. He dropped down next to her, breathing hard as he ran his hand over her, checking for any broken bones.

'You are the craziest woman I have ever met,' he grated. 'You could have been hurt.'

'I don't care.' Erin scrubbed her wet face with her hand and glared at him. 'Kazim is my son, and I won't leave him.'

Zahir shook his head impatiently. '*Why* do you want him? You have Ingledean, and my brother's fortune. What further use can Kazim be to you?'

'*I love him,*' Erin yelled. 'What do I have to do to make you believe that I don't care about the house or the money? You can have them. I'll sign over my inheritance to you, and then maybe you'll finally understand that the only thing I care about is Kazim.'

*I am convinced that her love for Kazim is genuine.* Zahir recalled his father's words, and his eyes narrowed on Erin's tear-streaked face. She wasn't lying. Even he, hardened cynic that he was, could see that her desperation to be reunited with the little boy was not some ploy designed to persuade him to offer her more money. She'd said she would give up Ingledean and her inheritance, and he could no longer deny that whatever else she might be she was a truly devoted mother. But he could not simply drive her back to the palace. The situation was more complicated than she knew.

'Take me back with you,' she whispered, her eyes shimmering with tears. 'Please.'

'I can't.' Zahir jerked upright and reached down to help her to her feet. 'My father is aware that you fled from the palace with Kazim,' he said heavily. 'He also heard that we had been alone in my office and that you were later seen looking…' He paused fractionally and even in the dark Erin could see the tide of colour that ran the length of his cheekbones. 'Looking distressed. The King believes that I have dishonoured you simply by the fact that we met without the presence of a chaperone. To protect your honour and prevent further gossip in the palace he has decreed that I must make arrangements for you to return immediately to England. The only way you can continue to live at the palace,' he went on, when Erin opened her mouth to protest, 'is if you become my wife.'

Erin shook her head, as if she could somehow retrieve her sanity. But the grim expression on Zahir's face told her she wasn't losing her mind. He was deadly serious. 'I don't want to marry you,' she faltered, wondering if she had cracked a rib when she'd jumped from the car, because it suddenly hurt to breathe. 'And I'm quite sure you don't want to marry me. If you explained to your father that nothing happened between us, and that my...' she flushed '...my honour is intact, surely he would relent...?'

'No,' Zahir snapped with a finality that made her heart sink. 'Besides, I would be lying if I told the King that nothing happened between us. If we had not been interrupted I would have made love to you, and we both know it.' He shrugged his shoulders and stepped closer, his eyes suddenly gleaming with sexual promise.

In the velvet-soft silence of the desert Erin was acutely aware of him; of the way that his breathing had quickened, and the sensual heat that emanated from his lean, hard body.

'I would also be lying if I told my father that I did not want to marry you,' he murmured.

Erin gaped at the utter unexpectedness of his statement, and a quiver of longing ran through her. He couldn't possibly mean he had fallen in love with her, she told herself sternly. Fairytales were for children—and she didn't even *want* him to love her. Which was just as well, she acknowledged, as his next words swiftly put paid to her silly dreams.

'I cannot risk you ever trying to take Kazim again,' he said harshly. 'As my wife, I will know exactly what you are up to every hour of the day and night—particularly at night,' he added, his voice thickening with a primitive need he made no effort to disguise. 'You cannot deny the attraction between us, Erin—not now, and certainly not when you are in my arms. When I kiss you I know you share my hunger. And a mutual need for sexual satisfaction is as good a reason as any to get married,' he stated bluntly.

'You can't marry for…for sex,' Erin argued, desperately trying to quell the rush of sensual awareness that was making her heart race. 'What about love?'

Bisma had said that Zahir had been in love with the bride his father had chosen for him. She did not know why he had not married her, but surely it proved that he *could* fall in love with the right woman—and he'd made it clear that that woman was definitely not her.

Zahir's brows winged upwards in the look of haughty arrogance she knew so well. 'Love is a vastly overrated emotion, I've always thought,' he said coolly. 'But if you need another reason other than the fact that we practically combust whenever we're within five feet of one another, you can console yourself with the knowledge that we both love Kazim and we are both determined to be good parents to him.'

He reached out suddenly and caught her chin, tilting her face so that he could stare into her eyes. Erin immediately focused on his mouth, and her tongue darted out in unconscious invitation. She was facing the most serious decision of her life, but part of her wished he would stop talking and just kiss her senseless, before tugging her down onto the sand and making her his beneath the brilliant stars that studded the night sky.

A slow, satisfied smile curved Zahir's lips. 'You can always close your eyes and pretend that you've sacrificed yourself for Kazim when I make love to you every night,' he taunted. 'Or you can behave like an adult and admit that you want me as much as I want you—that way we'll have a lot more fun as we learn to pleasure each other.'

'Don't say things like that.' Erin felt the blood rush to her face as heat suffused her whole body. She was sure he was deliberately trying to shock her, but she could not quell the quiver of anticipation that his words evoked. 'Are you saying that if I did agree to become your wife you would expect us to have a proper marriage?' she queried shakily.

'Do you honestly believe we could last five minutes alone with each other without doing this?' he countered, lowering his head before she had time to react, and claiming her mouth in a hot, hungry kiss that demolished any thoughts she might have had of resisting him.

His lips parted hers with bold assurance, and his tongue slid firmly between them to explore her with an eroticism that left her trembling. From the moment he touched her Erin was lost to his skilled mastery. He believed she was experienced, and her eager response to him must reinforce that belief. He did not know that for Erin every thrust of his tongue inside her mouth, the sharp nip of his teeth on her earlobe and the sensuous glide of his lips against her throat, were new and wondrous and utterly irresistible. She could not fight the feelings he aroused in her that made her breasts ache for his touch and caused molten heat to pool between her thighs. From the moment she'd first seen him at Ingledean she had fallen under his spell, and every time he kissed her he enslaved her more.

She could feel the hard ridge of his manhood pushing in-sistently against her pelvis, and when he slid his hand down from her breast to her hip and then suddenly swung her into his arms, she thought for one frantic moment that he intended to lay her down on the sand and make love to her properly. Her stomach muscles clenched with a fevered longing she could no longer deny, but then dipped in disappointment when he carried her over to the four-by-four and dumped her on the front seat.

He rounded the car and jumped in beside her, then paused with his hand on the ignition key and stared at her, his expression shuttered. 'It's your choice, Erin,' he said harshly. 'Ahead lies Al Razir, and from there Ingledean, or you can agree to marry me and I'll take you back to the palace and Kazim.'

He sounded as if he couldn't care less which option she chose, and his uninterest stung Erin's already raw emotions. 'That isn't a choice, it's blackmail,' she said bitterly. She swallowed, and then said tightly, 'All right, I'll marry you. But I want you to understand that my decision is purely for Kazim's sake.'

Zahir fired the engine and turned the four-by-four back towards the palace. 'Just keep reminding yourself of that when you're writhing and begging beneath me, sweetheart,' he taunted her with a grin. And then he leaned across and dropped a stinging kiss on her lips, drowning her angry retort and leaving her silently seething for the journey back across the desert.

*[illegible faded text from previous page showing through]*

# CHAPTER SIX

THEY were married five days later. None of Zahir's numerous relatives, whom Erin had met at three lavish banquets in the run-up to the wedding, seemed surprised by the speed of the arrangements, or by Zahir's decision to marry his brother's widow.

'Everyone is so proud of Zahir for choosing to honour an old custom of Qubbah and take on the responsibility of Faisal's wife and child,' Princess Fatima, the oldest of King Kahlid's children had explained, when she sat with Erin during one of the dinners that lasted for many hours and courses. 'Zahir has earned a reputation as a playboy prince these past few years, and he preferred to live at his bachelor apartments abroad rather than here at the palace. My father is pleased that he is now prepared to do his duty and marry you.'

Fatima did not mean the words unkindly. Like Zahir's other two sisters, she was friendly and welcoming and seemed genuinely eager to be Erin's friend. But she lived in a culture where arranged marriages and duty towards family were expected, and it was clear she believed Erin should feel grateful that Zahir had decided to 'take her on'.

Even though she knew Zahir had only asked her to be his wife for Kazim's sake, the idea that he regarded marrying her as an unwelcome duty did nothing for Erin's self-confidence. And if he was anticipating fireworks in the bedroom as a consolation prize, he was going to be disappointed, she thought bleakly.

Since the night he had brought her back to the palace they had not been alone. Even when they had flown on his private jet to Dubai, for a shopping trip like no other Erin had ever experienced, they had been accompanied by Fatima, and a host of staff whose job had been to carry the dozens of bags of couture clothes, shoes and accessories that Zahir had insisted she must have for her new life as the wife of a prince.

Each night they had dined with the King or attended banquets held in their honour, and there had been no opportunity for Erin to reveal to her husband-to-be that, far from being the hot-between-the-sheets siren he was expecting, she was a virgin.

It was her own fault, she had brooded dismally on the morning of her wedding. She had lied to him, and he thought that she and Faisal had shared a 'normal' marriage. Amazingly, he had not realised the level of her inexperience even when he'd kissed her. She must be a quick learner, she decided ruefully. Either that or she was as morally deficient as her mother, because when she was in Zahir's arms nothing seemed more important than assuaging the burning need for sexual fulfilment that he aroused in her.

To her relief, the wedding was a simple, low-key event compared to the extravagant banquets during which she had been conscious of the curious stares of the hundreds of guests who had been keen to see Prince Zahir's future bride. The ceremony took place in one of the palace state rooms—a breathtakingly opulent room with a pink marble-tiled floor and walls inlaid with gold, and magnificent crystal chandeliers suspended from the ceiling, glistening like diamond tears.

Erin's heart was beating unnaturally fast when she entered the state room and walked on trembling legs to where Zahir was waiting for her beneath an ornate brocade canopy. She had assumed she would wear one of her new outfits—possibly the cream suit from one of the world's leading fashion houses that Zahir had insisted on buying without even glancing at the exorbitant price tag. But when she had emerged from her bathroom this morning—after drying her hair into a mass of red curls that rippled down her back—her maids had been waiting to dress her in a forget-me-not-blue silk caftan decorated with exquisite beading on the bodice and sleeves and fastened at the back with tiny hooks.

A rustle went through the assembled guests, and as heads turned to watch her her nerve almost gave way. For a few seconds she was tempted to turn tail and flee. But if she did not marry Zahir she would lose custody of Kazim—and marriage to the devil himself was preferable to that.

There was something incredibly sensual about the brush of the silk caftan against her thighs when she walked. It made her think of Zahir's hands stroking her skin, his lips pressing feather-light kisses down her throat to her breasts, and by the time she reached his side she was pink-cheeked and flustered. The sight of him in a bespoke charcoal-grey suit, white silk shirt and a burgundy and gold tie sent a tremor through her that she could not disguise from his eagle sharp eyes. He was awesome, and from the moment he clasped her hand she could not take her eyes from his—her voice little more than a whisper when she made the responses required of her.

The only reason she had married him was for Kazim, she reminded herself urgently. But when Zahir bent his head and captured her mouth in a fierce, possessive kiss that proclaimed her his wife, she parted her lips helplessly and welcomed the thrust of his tongue, her uninhibited response earning a low growl of satisfaction from him that warned her he would expect her total capitulation tonight.

'What do you mean, we're spending our honeymoon at your camp in the desert?' she demanded hours later, when the formal wedding feast was finally over and Zahir had escorted her out of the banqueting room while the guests waved them on their way and showered them with rose petals.

'Isn't it romantic? This is the beginning of your life together,' Fatima had whispered excitedly when she'd kissed Erin farewell, but although Erin forced a smile, inside she was quaking. Reality was intruding with a vengeance, and she was wondering just what she had got herself into.

'I assumed we would be staying here at the palace,' she faltered when Zahir led her not to his private quarters in the west wing—which would now be her home too—but out of the main doors and down the steps to a four-by-four parked on the drive. 'What about Kazim?' She glanced wildly around, as if expecting Bisma to appear with the toddler, even though she knew he was fast asleep in the nursery.

Zahir gave her an impatient look when he opened the car door and she did not immediately climb in. 'He will remain here with his nanny. He is completely happy with Bisma, and I'm sure he'll be fine without you for a week or so,' he added tersely.

Erin's jaw dropped. 'You're expecting me to camp out in the desert for *a week*—or maybe longer?' She stared at him in horror. 'And without Kazim?' The thought of spending so long in Zahir's exclusive company was frankly terrifying. 'What will we do all day?'

At that Zahir threw back his head and gave a shout of

laughter. Erin had only ever heard him laughing with Kazim, and she loved the warm, rich sound, the way his eyes crinkled at the corners with amusement. But his next words made her heart thump painfully in her chest.

'Sleep, I imagine,' he drawled, the gleam in his eyes turning from humour to something altogether more nerve-racking. 'We will be on our honeymoon, and we'll use the days to re-cuperate our strength from the night before and prepare our-selves for the night ahead. I may allow you out of bed long enough to swim in the pool,' he added lazily, 'but you will spend most of your time beneath me, or on top of me.'

His voice lowered to a husky growl that sent a quiver of reaction along Erin's spine. 'You can drop the act of maidenly virtue now,' he told her bluntly as he suddenly swept her into his arms and placed her in the four-by-four. 'Qubbah may be rooted in tradition, but I'm a modern guy and I'm happy to accept that you may have had lovers before you married my brother.'

Erin could swear she actually felt her heart plummet down to her toes, and she turned to stare at him with huge, troubled eyes when he jumped in next to her and fired the engine. She should never have lied to him, she thought frantically. 'Zahir…I have to tell you…'

'It's all right; I don't want a detailed list of your boy-friends.' Zahir swiftly cut her off.

Sure, he had a modern outlook, he assured himself. Women were equal to men, and they had just as much right to experi-ment with a variety of sex partners. He didn't understand why the idea of Erin making love with any other man filled him with such savage fury. He should be pleased that she was sexually experienced, and tonight he would use every ounce of his own skill and passion to make love to her. He would teach her things that would no doubt shock her, and he would give her more pleasure than she had ever experienced—until he had driven all memories of her previous lovers from her mind for good and she thought only of him.

'But, Zahir…'

'Leave it, Erin. I have no wish to rake over your past or list all the women who've shared *my* bed. It would take most of the night,' he added with a self-satisfied grin, 'and I have other plans for us tonight.'

After that they drove through the desert in a silence that stretched Erin's nerves to snapping point. Eventually they reached an oasis. A distinctive Bedouin tent loomed out of the darkness, pitched beneath several palm trees and illuminated by flickering oil lamps. Moonlight dappled the inky surface of a large natural pool, and more stars than Erin had ever imagined existed studded the sky like pins in a velvet pincushion.

Some distance away she could see more tents and, following her gaze, Zahir explained, 'Servants' quarters. But I don't have many staff here, and they are under strict orders not to disturb us.'

He held out his arms to assist her down from the four-by-four, and despite her misgivings the brief contact with his body was enough to send heat coursing through Erin's veins. The feel of his silk shirt beneath her fingertips and the sensual musk of his cologne captivated her senses, and her legs felt weak. When he opened the tent flap she stared around at the jumbled array of brightly coloured cushions and patterned rugs, and at the vast, low bed set beneath a billowing canopy and draped with a satin coverlet.

It was like something out of an Arabian fantasy, and if this had been a real marriage, born of love rather than convenience, she would have adored the romantic setting. But Zahir had married her out of duty and because he wanted to have sex with her, and the knowledge that he was expecting her to join him on that huge bed made her feel as though she had turned into her mother. She was no better than a whore—for what difference did it make that she had agreed to barter her body in return for remaining with Kazim rather than hard cash?

The panic that had been building inside her since the wedding ceremony had increased tenfold on the drive from the palace, and now threatened to overwhelm her. Her voice was sharp and high-pitched when she cried, 'I'm not sleeping with you.'

'Sleeping was not what *I* had in mind either,' Zahir drawled lazily. He strolled over to a table and lifted a bottle of champagne from an ice bucket. 'I can think of many infinitely more enjoyable ways of spending my wedding night.'

He filled two glasses and offered one to Erin, but she shook her head and wrapped her arms tightly around her body. It was warm inside the tent, but her teeth were chattering and she felt horribly sick. She had only picked at the wedding feast, so her nausea was not likely to be caused by something she'd eaten. It was fear, plain and simple, she acknowledged, her eyes fixed on Zahir, and her breath caught in her throat when he began to unfasten his shirt buttons. The sight of his golden skin, overlaid with a covering of fine black hairs, and the visible ridges of his abdominal muscles shattered the last remnants of her self-control.

'I mean it. This whole charade was a mistake.'

'Charade?' He frowned slightly but was not distracted from shrugging his shirt over his shoulders and allowing it to drop to the floor.

'Our *marriage*,' Erin said wildly. 'It was a mistake and I

should never have agreed to it. You used Kazim to blackmail me, and that was a *despicable* thing to do.'

Even to her own ears she sounded close to hysteria, but she couldn't help it. Stripped to his waist, Zahir was a demi-god who made her mouth run dry—but he was expecting a night of tempestuous passion with a woman he believed was an expert in the art of seduction. He would probably laugh if she asked him to be gentle, and think it was all part of a game she was playing. But her 'maidenly virtue' wasn't an act, and wild horses would not force her into his bed.

'I'll sleep over at the servants' quarters,' she told him, hastily dropping her gaze when she caught the gleam of anger in his eyes.

To her surprise Zahir made no attempt to stop her when she wrenched the tent flap open, but his murmured, 'Watch out for snakes,' stopped her in her tracks.

'What snakes?'

'Cobras, mainly, and the odd horned viper—their venom is deadly, of course, but I'm sure you'll be fine as long as you look where you are putting your feet.'

'But it's dark. I won't be able to see them.' Erin cast a nervous glance out at the inky blackness of the desert and wondered what lurked in its mysterious shadows. Did snakes move around at night?

A faint rustling sound from a nearby bush caused her heart to practically leap from her chest, and she shrieked and jumped back inside the tent, her overwrought emotions boiling over into explosive temper when she caught sight of Zahir's smirk.

'I'm glad you find the situation so funny!' Suddenly she was incandescent with rage. She was tired of being manipulated, tired of being backed into a corner, and with a cry of fury she snatched up the nearest object to hand—a small glazed bowl set on a low table—and flung it at him. 'I must have been temporarily insane when I agreed to be your wife, but my sanity has returned and I want a divorce.'

With lightning reactions Zahir caught the bowl and set it down before striding towards her, his expression darkening from amusement to anger and his eyes glittering with a primitive hunger that caused Erin's heart to pound. 'Oh, no,' he growled as he reached her and tangled his fingers in her hair when she turned to run. '*This* is what you want, my little wildcat—you just don't have the guts to admit it.'

He jerked her against his chest and bent her backwards until she was sure her spine would snap. Her eyes widened in fearful anticipation when he lowered his head to hers.

'I saw the furtive glances you gave me during the wedding feast, the hungry longing in your gaze that you thought I hadn't noticed,' he said harshly, his warm breath whispering across her lips. 'I know you were imagining us together, our naked bodies pressed skin against skin, your limbs entwined with mine. And tonight it is time to turn the fantasy into reality. I will make you mine,' he promised; his voice thick with a sexual promise that caused a mixture of apprehension and undeniable excitement to run through her. 'I don't know what's caused this sudden change of heart. Maybe the wedding brought back memories of my brother. But you agreed to marry me of your own free will, and after tonight you will be in no doubt that you are *my* wife now, not Faisal's.'

Erin's cry of protest was lost beneath the fierce pressure of Zahir's kiss. His tongue forced access into the moist warmth of her mouth, parting her lips with barely controlled savagery and exploring her with such skilled eroticism that she was powerless to fight him or the tumultuous emotions he aroused in her. He was her prince, the man of her dreams, powerful, formidable, a man who would sweep away the barriers she had built around herself and discover the intensely sensual part of her that she had tried so hard to suppress.

She wondered vaguely why he had sounded so harsh when he had mentioned Faisal. She might almost believe he resented the fact that she had been married to his brother. But she must surely have imagined the note of raw jealousy in his voice.

'This was inevitable from the moment we first saw each other at Ingledean House,' he grated, when he finally broke the kiss and stared down at her swollen mouth, his dark eyes gleaming with a determination that made Erin tremble. 'I knew the instant I saw you that I wanted you in my bed,' he told her with brutal honesty. 'I assumed you were the maid, and instead of thinking about my dead brother I could not stop myself from planning how quickly I could seduce you.

'Now that time has come, and I intend to make love to you until you plead for my possession and can think of no other man but me,' he promised arrogantly, lifting her suddenly into his arms and striding over to the bed. 'You have tormented my dreams for too long,' he muttered as he set her down on her feet and spun her round so that he could unfasten the row of tiny hooks that ran down the back of her wedding gown. 'And I know that you share my hunger, *kalila*. Your body does not lie—see.'

She still had her back to him as he pushed the silk caftan over her shoulders, tracing his mouth along the fragile line of her collarbone while his hands came round to cup her pale bare breasts in his palms. Her dusky pink nipples had already tightened into hard peaks, betraying the molten desire that was flooding through her veins, and she could not restrain a soft moan when he captured her nipples between his fingers and gently tugged, sending exquisite flames of sensation from her breasts to the damp heat between her thighs.

The caftan fluttered to the floor, and Erin caught her breath when Zahir turned her to him and she saw the look of primitive, feral hunger blazing in his eyes.

'You are the most beautiful woman I have ever known,' he said thickly, as he took the combs from her hair and ran his fingers through the rippling mass of vibrant, silky curls. She was a siren, and he could not resist the exquisite combination of flame-coloured hair and smoky grey eyes that were no longer flashing with temper but dark and soft with desire.

He had wed her reluctantly, but he did not share that same reluctance to bed her, he brooded as he stared down at her slender body, and at the tiny scrap of white lace that shielded her femininity from his eyes. His desperate desire for her was shaming, but now she was his wife and he did not have to fight it any longer. Instead he would give in to this elemental need to part her soft white thighs and plunge his agonisingly aroused shaft deep into her, to take them both to the heights of sexual ecstasy until he was utterly sated—and then perhaps he would be able to get on with his life and relegate her to a distant corner of his mind.

She was staring up at him, her pupils dilated so that her eyes seemed too big in her delicate, fine-boned face. The sight of her pink tongue darting out to trace her lower lip drew a muttered imprecation from him as he lifted her and placed her on the bed, immediately covering her body with his own. He wanted her now, hard and fast, he acknowledged, as he tugged her knickers down her legs and slid his hand between her thighs. He wanted her with a primitive hunger that was rapidly spiralling out of control—and he couldn't wait.

Erin gasped at the feel of Zahir's hard arousal straining beneath his trousers and nudging into her thigh. His naked torso pressed down on her so that she was aware of the faint abrasion of his chest hair brushing against her breasts. Somewhere at the back of her mind a small voice was telling her she should stop him, but the temptation to run her hands over the bunched muscles of his upper arms and then lower, to his chest and flat stomach, was too strong to resist.

He kissed her again, his lips warm and firm on hers but no longer seeking to dominate. Instead he slid his tongue into her mouth and initiated a slow, unhurried exploration that drugged her senses, so that she curled her arms around his neck and kissed him back with a fervour that drew a groan from deep in his throat. At last he lifted his head and stared down at her, his eyes hooded and slumberous. He supported himself on his elbows and moved his head down to her breast, flicking his tongue across her nipple until it swelled and tightened and then drawing it fully into his mouth and sucking her until she moaned and tossed her head restlessly from side to side.

'Please,' she whimpered, past caring that he had reduced her to a pliant, submissive sex slave. She was on fire, so desperate for him to continue his wicked sorcery that she slid her fingers into his silky black hair and tugged his head to her other breast.

'Your eagerness is *such* a turn-on,' he taunted her, his eyes glinting with amusement when her cheeks flooded with colour.

She wasn't supposed to be eager—she was supposed to be fighting him, she acknowledged sickly. The note of smug satisfaction in his voice filled her with shame at her weakness, but the tug of his mouth on her other nipple was so exquisite that she arched her back and pushed her knuckle into her mouth to stifle her scream of pleasure.

Now he was moving his head lower, trailing his mouth over her flat stomach and pausing to dip his tongue into her navel before continuing down. His warm breath stirred the tight cluster of red-gold curls between her thighs and she tensed, her eyes widening with shock when he gently parted the swollen outer lips of her femininity and pushed his tongue delicately between them to discover the sticky wetness within.

'Zahir!' She couldn't believe what he was doing. Not even her wildest fantasies had included him bestowing upon her this most intimate caress, but his invasive tongue had found the sensitive nub of her clitoris and she could feel little spasms of pleasure building inside her.

Just when she was sure she could stand no more, he lifted his head and rolled off her, his huge chest heaving and his face a taut mask as he stood to remove his trousers and then tugged his silk boxers down to reveal the jutting length of his fully aroused manhood. Time seemed to stand still, and she stared at him in wordless apprehension. But the time to stop him had long passed, and she knew from the stark hunger in his midnight-dark gaze that there could only be one outcome—his total and absolute possession.

Paralysed with fearful anticipation, she did not resist when he pushed her thighs apart and came down on her, positioning himself between them. He moved his hands under her bottom and lifted her to receive him, his eyes locked with hers as he rubbed his thick, swollen shaft up and down her moist opening.

'This is what I wanted the moment I laid eyes on you at

Ingledean,' he told her rawly, 'when I fantasised about spreading you across the desk and plunging into you.'

And as he spoke he matched his words with the deed, easing forward to penetrate her with one deep, powerful thrust that drew a shocked gasp from her as she was forced to accept the awesome length of his erection.

Erin's sharp cry was born of shock rather than pain. She was so aroused that her vaginal muscles quickly stretched to accommodate him, but the feel of his pulsing length pushing deeper into her was startlingly new, and her breath came in shallow pants as her body slowly relaxed and absorbed his male strength.

Zahir had stilled when he felt the unmistakable barrier of her virginity, and at his hoarsely muttered, 'How is this possible?' her eyes flew open and met his stunned gaze.

She felt him ease back, as if he was going to withdraw from her, but now that the first moments of panic were over she was starting to enjoy the way he filled her so completely, and she wrapped her legs around him and urged him forward again. Her muscles were contracting in sharp, pleasurable little jerks, and with an instinct as old as time she began to move her hips against him.

She heard him growl something in Arabic as he lost the battle waging inside him and matched her movements. His hands settled on her hips and he thrust into her again and again, establishing a pulsing rhythm with deep, steady strokes that created the most incredible sensations inside her. The pleasure was so intense that she lost track of who she was and became a wanton creature, responding to him with mindless passion as she dug her nails into his shoulders and then slid her hands down and cupped his buttocks, urging him to thrust faster, deeper, to take her to the edge of some unknown place.

Surely her body would explode with pleasure? Surely it was not possible to withstand any more? But still it built, and still he drove into her, while she tossed her head from side to side, her mind, her body, her whole being concentrated on the exquisite sensations he was arousing deep in her pelvis which were now reaching a crescendo.

'Zahir…' She sobbed his name over and over, her pride long since discarded. He was her master and she his willing slave. And suddenly she was there, suspended for timeless seconds on the edge of ecstasy, before he drove into her again and she felt herself falling as her body convulsed with an intense pleasure that was beyond anything she had ever imagined.

Even then, when she was writhing beneath him, he did not stop, but increased his pace, thrusting into her hard and fast, the corded muscles of his neck and shoulders standing out as he sought to retain control. And then, with a savage groan dragged from the depths of his soul, his control splintered spectacularly and he threw back his head, his eyes closed and his jaw clenched, as he pumped his seed into her before collapsing on top of her, his chest heaving as he snatched air into his lungs.

She should have expected such barely leashed, violent and primitive passion from a desert prince, Erin thought numbly as she lay beneath him, his weight pressing her into the mattress and his heart slamming beneath her fingertips. Her sanity was slowly returning and she was appalled—not by his fierce hunger, but by her unrestrained response to him.

Deep down she had clung to a fantasy of one day giving her heart and her body to the man she loved, who loved her in return, but instead she had been powerless to resist Zahir's wildfire passion. She had given no thought to love or respect. Her only consideration had been to assuage the desperate need he had aroused in her. But now, in the aftermath of that passion, she was able to view her behaviour dispassionately, and she felt deeply ashamed.

At last he rolled off her and lay on his side, propped up on one elbow, his dark eyes unfathomable as he stared down at her. Too embarrassed to meet his gaze, Erin attempted to scramble off the bed. But her efforts to escape him were thwarted when he caught her arm and dragged her back down beside him.

'You were a virgin.' It wasn't a question but an aggressive statement, and only then, as she watched his eyes harden to chips of obsidian, did she realise the extent of his anger. 'How come, Erin?' he demanded harshly. 'Although I don't really need to ask,' he added with undisguised disgust. 'You actually had me fooled the night I rescued you from the desert. I really believed your motive for marrying Faisal and adopting Kazim was because you loved them both. But it's obvious you persuaded my brother to marry you, and make you the only beneficiary of his will, and then reneged on your marital vows. Faisal was sick—he was dying,' he grated bitterly. 'But you already had what you wanted. You knew you stood to inherit Ingledean, and you couldn't even make the last months of his life happy by being a proper wife to him.'

With another furious oath he swung his legs over the edge of the bed and jumped to his feet, as if he could not bear to be near her. He had received the biggest shock of his life when he'd discovered that she was a virgin, and he was still struggling with the realisation that he was her first lover. And mixed with shock was another feeling that he was ashamed to admit—a ridiculous feeling of elation and primitive possessiveness. The corrosive envy that had besieged him every time he thought of her with Faisal had disappeared, and now he even felt sympathy for his brother.

'Why didn't you tell me?' he demanded harshly. When she did not reply he continued, 'I can only assume you didn't because you realised that if you had admitted you were a virgin I would have had proof that your marriage to Faisal was a sham and you *had* done as I'd first suspected and married him for his money. If I had then refused to consummate our marriage and demanded an annulment, you would have stood to lose all the things you *really* care about—Ingledean, the fortune you inherited from my brother, and your position as the wife of a billionaire.'

He broke off and gave a grim laugh. 'Did you honestly think I wouldn't notice the indisputable proof of your innocence? It's possible I hurt you.' His conscience burned when he recalled how he had taken her, with a distinct lack of finesse. 'But you only have yourself to blame if I did,' he growled, guilt adding to his inexplicable fury that he had in some way ruined a moment that should have been special—for both of them. 'Perhaps you concluded that all you were gaining financially was worth a few moments of discomfort?' he added scathingly.

'No. You've got it all wrong,' Erin cried frantically, pushing her tangled curls out of her eyes as she jerked upright, and then blushing scarlet when his eyes settled on her bare breasts. To her horror her nipples immediately hardened to provocative peaks, and smothering a groan of mortification she dragged the silk bedcover around her before she lifted her head to him.

Only moments ago Zahir had taken her to heaven. Now he was looking at her as if she was the lowest life-form on the planet. 'I admit I lied about the details of my marriage,' she choked, wishing that instead of putting her on trial the minute he had withdrawn his body from hers, he had taken her in his arms and stroked her hair, made her feel that giving her virginity to him had been something to cherish. 'You're right. I was afraid that if you knew I had been Faisal's wife in name only, you would have used it as leverage to take Kazim from me. But Faisal never *wanted* me to be his proper wife,' she explained urgently. 'He only ever loved one woman, and he spoke about Maryam until the day he died.

'When he was told that he was dying he asked me to marry him purely so that I could adopt Kazim as quickly as possible. And because I believed that Kazim had no one else to bring him up, I agreed. I don't have a family. My mother died when I was young and I spent the rest of my childhood in care. I would have done anything to prevent the same thing happening to Kazim,' she said quietly. 'And I told you right from the start that my only reason for marrying *you* was so that I could stay at the palace with him.'

For the first time in his life Zahir did not know what to think. Part of him wanted to believe she was telling the truth, but the cynic in him pointed out that it was highly unlikely she had adopted Kazim without wanting anything in return. But what did it matter if her motives had been questionable? She was his wife now—in word and deed. He had married her because he had been desperate to bed her, and, despite being a virgin, her passion had matched his.

Marriages had succeeded on less, he brooded as he strode back over to the bed, his eyes narrowing when Erin immediately clutched the satin bedspread to her. 'You say that the only reason you married me was so that you could stay with

Kazim. But if that's so why didn't you stop me making love to you tonight?'

He dropped down onto the mattress and idly wound one of her silky red curls around his finger. Then, before she had time to react, he whipped the bedspread from her grasp and pushed her flat on her back.

Her eyes were huge in her flushed face, and he watched with satisfaction the way her pupils dilated when he skimmed his hand over her stomach and cupped one small, creamy breast in his palm. Her breath was coming in sharp little gasps, her lips slightly parted, pink and lush and seriously tempting. 'You surrendered your innocence to me, *kalila*, and I can only think it was because you were overwhelmed by the passion I aroused in you and couldn't deny yourself the sexual release your body craved.'

'Well, of course you would think that, wouldn't you? Because your ego is so over-inflated I'm surprised you don't need to wear gravity boots,' Erin muttered through gritted teeth, incensed by his arrogance and her pathetic, shaming inability to resist him.

The brush of his thumb-pad over her swollen nipple was so exquisite that she had to bite her lip to hold back her betraying moan of pleasure, but fortunately her pride had at last woken up, and she would rather die than let him see how much he affected her.

'Actually, your first assumption was right. I knew that if I told you I was a virgin you would realise that my marriage to Faisal had been in name only and there was a chance you could win custody of Kazim. But now I am your wife—our marriage has been consummated, and even under Qubbah's archaic laws I must have rights to my son. I hate to disabuse you of the notion that you're irresistible, and that sex with you is fantastic,' she continued, dropping her gaze when she saw the flash of anger in his dark eyes, 'but I'm afraid I'm in no hurry to repeat the experience.'

The ensuing silence played havoc with her nerves, so she faked a yawn and pulled the bedspread over her once more, praying he would go and find somewhere else to sleep.

'Really?' Zahir said at last, in a deceptively soft tone that sent a shaft of nervous apprehension down her spine. 'My apologies, *kalila*, I had not realised that you were so reluctant. Indeed,' he drawled silkily, 'from your screams of pleasure I was sure you were enjoying every caress and kiss and bite—but let's see, shall we, just how much you hate it when I touch you…here?'

Erin drew a swift, shallow breath when he flicked the bedspread aside and pushed his hand between her thighs, parting them with insulting ease. 'Let me up, Zahir,' she grated, every muscle in her body clenched as she fought the insidious warmth that was already flooding through her veins. 'I don't want this. So unless you intend to take me by force—' She broke off, her heart thudding erratically, when stroked his finger lazily up and down the swollen outer lips of her femininity and then probed between them, exploring her so thoroughly that it was all she could do not to lift her hips in mute supplication. She could feel the betraying wetness pooling between her legs, and could not control the first delicious spasms that racked her when he stretched her wider and inserted another finger, while his thumb-pad found the ultra-sensitive nub of her clitoris and brushed, feather-light, across it.

When he lowered his head to her breasts and drew first one dusky pink crest and then its twin into his mouth she stifled a moan, From somewhere she dredged enough will-power to brace her hands against his shoulders and attempt to push him away. 'Don't.' But her frantic plea was lost beneath the pressure of his mouth as he captured her lips in a bruising kiss that sought to dominate and prove that he was in control.

His lips were hot and hard, his tongue tormenting her relentlessly as he thrust deep into her mouth in an erotic simulation of lovemaking. Her determination to fight him was fading, lost in the maelstrom of sensation he was arousing with his mouth and his wickedly invasive fingers.

'I have never taken a woman by force in my life, and I don't intend to start with you,' Zahir growled against her skin. 'Tell me now that you don't want this and I'll stop,' he taunted, his eyes gleaming with undisguised mockery when she opened her mouth but could not utter the words. 'Do you want me to stop, Erin?'

'*No.*' The word was wrenched from her soul, and she squeezed her eyes shut to blot out his satisfied smile as he moved over her. She was utterly humiliated by her weakness, but she was on fire for him, her body trembling with her desperate need to feel him inside her.

'What *do* you want?' He was hovering mere inches from her, the hard ridge of his erection pushing into her belly. He was determined to have her complete capitulation, and she gave a sob of shamed despair.

'You.'

He entered her with a hard, savage thrust, withdrew almost fully and thrust again, deep, powerful strokes that filled her to the hilt and drove every thought from her mind but the thundering urgency to reach that magical place he had taken her to only minutes before. She realised that when he had

made love to her for the first time and discovered her innocence he must have tempered his passion to accommodate her
inexperience. But now she was no longer a virgin, and he took
her with an almost brutal force, powering into her so that she
simply anchored her nails into his shoulders and clung on for
the wildest ride of her life.

They climaxed together, a violent, soul-shattering explosion that saw her rake her nails down his back as her body
shook with the intensity of her release and caused him to
mutter something in Arabic, his voice low and raw.

His chest was heaving when he rolled off her immediately
the last spasms of his passion had died away. He stood to drag
his trousers on and stared down at her dispassionately, his eyes
darkening as they lingered on the faint bruises on her pale skin.

'Brute,' Erin muttered thickly, tears of mortification
burning her eyes.

She hated him, and hated herself more. Yet even now, when
he was looking down his arrogant nose at her as if she was a
whore and he had just paid for her services, she longed to trace
her fingers over the hard planes of his face and feel the brush
of his lips on hers in a kiss of tenderness rather than blazing
passion. From the first moment she had seen him she had felt
a connection with him that she did not understand—as if their
souls were inextricably linked and only he could ease the
loneliness that had haunted her all her life. It couldn't be love,
she told herself desperately. It wasn't possible to love and hate
someone simultaneously—was it? And if it *was* love, then she
was an even bigger fool than she had believed—because Zahir
was as harsh and unforgiving as the desert. His heart was hewn
from granite, and he would never love her.

At last he snatched up his shirt and strolled over to the tent flap, pausing briefly to glance back at her—still spread on the satin bedcover with her hair tumbling in fiery disarray around her shoulders. 'Never tell me again that you don't want me,' he warned softly, his black eyes boring into her as if he could see inside her head. 'Because now we both know it's not true.' And with that he dipped his head in a mocking salute and stepped outside into the desert.

# CHAPTER SEVEN

PALE rays of sunlight filtered through the tent flap and slanted across Zahir's face, rousing him from sleep. As always, he was instantly alert, and turned his head to find Erin curled up next to him, her glorious hair spread like a fiery halo about her head.

Last night when he had joined her in bed, long after she had fallen asleep, he had been struck by how young she looked—and how innocent. Her pillow had been drenched, and the streaks of tears on her cheeks had tugged hard on his conscience. Usually he had no patience with women's tears, but Erin had cried alone and silently—he had been standing just outside the tent and hadn't heard her—and the idea that she had sobbed herself to sleep had forced him to evaluate his treatment of her.

It was nothing to be proud of, he'd acknowledged as he had stretched out beneath the sheets and tried to ignore the fact that she was lying inches from him, her delectable body barely concealed beneath the sheer grey silk chemise she must have donned after he had stormed out of the tent. Now, in the light of a new day, he was besieged by a nagging sense of shame.

She was no longer innocent. He had taken her virginity with as much finesse as a barbarian. It was impossible to believe he had not hurt her, and the thought filled him with such bitter self-disgust that he flipped back the sheet and swung his legs over the edge of the bed, raking his hand wearily through his hair. Whatever Erin might have done in the past, she had not deserved such brutality, and the fact that she had responded to him so fervently did not excuse his behaviour.

He was suddenly conscious that the rhythmic sound of her breathing had changed, and he glanced round to find her watching him with big, wary grey eyes. For the first time in his life he did not know what to say. None of the usual glib compliments that formed part of his practised routine when he woke with a woman in his bed came to his lips. The silence ached with emotions he did not understand, with a faint feeling of regret he felt helpless to express, and yet despite his self-loathing he could not tear his eyes from her face.

She was his woman, his wife, and his desire for her this morning was, if possible, even more intense than last night. But he would have to control the fire that licked in his veins and had already caused him to harden in eager anticipation. He had vowed in the pre-dawn hours when he'd stalked restlessly in front of the tent that he would not touch her again until she'd indicated that she wanted him to. He would not force himself on her like a coarse boor. He was a prince, for heaven's sake, and it was time he exerted some of the iron self-control for which he was renowned.

'I need to apologise for last night,' he said stiffly, his clipped tone shattering the uneasy quiet.

Erin's eyes widened even further. 'For what last night? For making love to me?'

He could feel her surprise—as if an apology was the last thing she had expected—and his jaw clenched. 'I was rough with you,' he grated. Apologies were not easy, but this one had to be made. 'I have spent the past week anticipating our wedding night, and my impatience made me careless. By the time I discovered it was your first time it was too late to restrain my hunger for you. If you had told me—' He broke off, clearly struggling to contain his impatience. 'If I had known, I would have acted differently—been gentler,' he expounded at her confused frown.

'If you had known I was a virgin you wouldn't have made love to me at all,' Erin murmured. 'You would have had our marriage annulled and asked the courts to award you custody of Kazim—wouldn't you?' she added uncertainly.

Zahir's gaze meshed with hers, and the tension between them changed subtly as awareness wove its sensual spell. 'Kazim was not the only reason I married you,' he said harshly. 'And you credit me with more self-control than I possess—certainly where you are concerned. The knowledge that you were a virgin would not have lessened my desire for you,' he said with a self-derisive laugh, 'but I would not have forced myself on you like some clumsy youth at the mercy of his hormones.'

Erin watched in fascination as dull colour highlighted his incredible cheekbones. Zahir was a royal prince, and fiercely proud, but previously she had mistaken his pride for arrogance and hated him for it—or so she had tried to kid herself, she thought ruefully. With a sigh she rolled onto her back and stared up at the canopy of rich burgundy silk that was draped above the bed. 'You didn't force me,' she said flatly. 'I wanted you as much as you wanted me.'

Colour stole into her own cheeks as she recalled her wanton behaviour last night, the way she had practically begged him to make love to her. If anyone should feel ashamed it was her. But her pride seemed to have deserted her for good, and she only wished he would lie back down, next to her, and work his magic on her eager body once more.

But, far from reassuring him, her words seemed to anger him—although she had a strange feeling that he was angry with himself rather than with her. He jumped to his feet and paced the floor of the tent—all powerful, muscle-packed masculinity, with his bare chest gilded from the morning light, a pair of thin cotton trousers tied with a drawstring around his waist.

'Your honesty humbles me,' he said tersely. 'Nevertheless, I am not proud of my behaviour on our wedding night, and I want you to understand that you have not married a brute intent only on his own selfish pleasure. I will wait until you feel ready to share my bed again, and when that time comes I will temper my desire and make sure you are fully aroused and ready for me before I make love to you.'

Just the thought of him ensuring that she was 'fully aroused' was having a profound effect on her, Erin thought frantically, feeling her breasts tingle in anticipation of his touch. And she didn't want him to temper his desire; she wanted him to kiss her in all the places he had explored last night, especially the secret, silken heat between her thighs, and then move over her and enter her with the hard, rhythmic thrusts that she already seemed to be addicted to.

Zahir had been prowling the tent like a caged tiger, but now he came over to the bed and stared down at her, his keen gaze taking in the hectic flush that stained her cheeks. He had told her he would not make love to her again until she was ready, but the gleam of undisguised sexual hunger in his eyes made her long to throw back the sheet and tell him she was ready now, this minute, and couldn't wait.

'I am aware that we had little opportunity to get to know each other in the days before our wedding,' Zahir muttered abruptly, forcing himself to step away from the bed.

Despite all his good intentions, Erin was an irresistible temptation, lying there with her hair tumbling in silky disarray over her shoulders, the firm swell of her breasts visible above the neckline of her chemise, beckoning him to slide the strap down so that the deliciously soft mounds spilled into his hands. He strode over to the tent flap and unfastened it, so that more sunlight poured through the gap, standing with his back to her so that she would not see the confusing whirl of emotions in his face.

'I would like to know more about you,' he told her, realising with a jolt of surprise that it was the truth, and not simply a ploy to take his mind off his need to make love to her. 'You said last night that you had been desperate to prevent Kazim growing up in care, as you had done after the death of your mother. How old were you when she died?'

'Ten,' Erin replied unemotionally. She sensed that Zahir was waiting for her to continue, but she had no wish to revisit her past. She tried to keep the memories of her childhood locked away, but images floated into her mind of the squalid flat that had been her home for her early years, of her mother, painfully thin, with long red hair that hung lank around her pinched, white face. She still had a clear picture in her head of Jeannie Maguire's unhealthy pallor, the dull eyes that had seemed sunken into her skull, and her expression of blank uninterest in anything other than her need for her next fix.

Zahir was staring at her, clearly curious. 'Was she killed

in an accident?' he queried, and the unexpected gentleness in his voice brought a lump to her throat.

He was a prince who had grown up in a world of unimaginable luxury—he could have no comprehension of her deprived childhood, when her mother's addiction to hard drugs had meant Erin had frequently gone hungry for both food and basic care.

'She was ill.' The social worker who'd been appointed after Jeannie's death had said that drug addiction was a disease, but Zahir did not need to know the sordid details. Like how her mother had paid for the drugs by prostituting herself.

'And after she died, was there no one in the family who could have cared for you?'

'She didn't have a family.' Erin hesitated, and then added, 'She told me once that she had run away from home when she was fifteen, after her stepfather abused her. I don't know any other details, and Social Services never traced any relatives who might have taken me in. I know you suspect my motives for adopting Kazim, but I swear my only reason was because I believed he had no one else who would love him. And to a child love is more important than anything,' she finished huskily.

Zahir felt something tug at his insides. He had been a similar age to Erin when his mother had left Qubbah, and he had never forgotten how badly he had missed her. He'd been lucky that he'd still had his father and brother and sisters around him, but Erin had had no one.

He had convinced himself that she was a heartless gold-digger because it had suited him, he acknowledged grimly. It had been the only weapon at his disposal to fight his ferocious attraction to her. But what if he had been wrong about her? What if she really *had* adopted Kazim so that she could give him the love she had been denied during her childhood? It made his treatment of her seem even worse—particularly the way he had trapped her in a marriage she hadn't wanted, simply because of his selfish determination to take her to bed.

'You told my father that you loved Faisal,' he muttered, voicing the thought that had been gnawing at him. 'But you must have been lying. Because last night I proved conclusively that you were never a proper wife to him.'

'I did love him,' Erin insisted. 'As a brother and my best friend.' She gave a faint smile. 'Faisal trusted me at a time when no one else would. I had been sacked from my first job as nanny to two little girls because I'd refused to sleep with their father. Mr Fitzroy told everyone that he'd had to fire me because I flirted with him and begged him for an affair.' She wrinkled her nose in disgust. 'He was old enough to be my father, for heaven's sake. The employment agency refused to keep me on their books, and I was afraid I'd never get another job. But Faisal believed me. He employed me to look after his baby son, and I'm so glad he did—because I fell in love with Kazim at first sight.'

The silence that followed her last statement seemed to stretch interminably, but at last Zahir turned his head and stared at her. 'So Kazim really is the reason you married me?' he said, in a casual tone that disguised an overwhelming urge to slam his fist into a punchball for as many times as it took to relieve the tight knot of anger that had formed inside him. 'You were a sacrificial virgin in every sense, weren't you?' he murmured sardonically. 'But even though I now accept that your love for Kazim is genuine, I will never let him go. You accuse me of blackmailing you into marriage, but last night you wanted me, Erin—and, as I have already said, desire is as good a basis for marriage as anything. Particularly when it is combined with our mutual determination to give Kazim a happy and loving childhood.'

He had walked back over to the bed, and Erin gasped when he suddenly whipped back the sheet and swept her up into his arms. 'We have a duty to Kazim to make our marriage work,' he told her as he strode out of the tent. 'I rushed you last night, perhaps even frightened you.' He frowned blackly at the thought. 'But I am prepared to be patient and give you time to adjust to married life.'

Despite the early hour the sun was hot, and Erin blinked in its brilliant glare when Zahir set her down on a flat rock by the edge of the pool. She wasn't sure what he wanted from her, and her confusion increased when he casually untied the cord around his waist and let his trousers fall to the floor.

'What are you *doing*?' she demanded in a strangled voice. Last night she had been too absorbed in the feel of his warm, satiny skin sliding against hers to look at him properly, but the sight of his body revealed in all its muscled glory beneath the bright sunlight made her heart stop. She had never even seen a man completely naked before, but Zahir was a truly magnificent specimen of masculinity, and she longed to reach out and stroke her fingers over his golden skin.

'I told you I would let you out of bed occasionally to swim,' he drawled, amusement glinting in his eyes at her stunned expression. He turned and stepped into the crystal clear pool, affording her a tantalising glimpse of his taut buttocks before he glanced back at her and held out his hand, 'Are you going to join me?'

'I didn't bring a swimsuit.' She knew she was staring at him, but she could not drag her eyes from the formidable width of his chest, the whorls of dark hair that arrowed down over his flat stomach, and lower still…

'As you can see, neither did I.' He saw her glance anxiously towards the staff quarters and smiled. 'No one can see us through the trees, and the servants will not disturb us.' His smile faded and he added seriously, 'You're quite safe with me, Erin. I gave my word that I will not lay a finger on you and I will abide by that promise.'

'What a pity.' The words spilt from her lips and she immediately blushed scarlet, but when he tensed and gave her a questioning stare she held his gaze, her heart thudding at the flare of undisguised hunger in his eyes. He had always been honest about his reasons for marrying her: he wanted Kazim to live at the palace and he wanted her in his bed. Now it was time for her to be honest too.

He had fascinated her from the moment she had met him at Ingledean, and when he had made love to her last night she had proved that she was utterly incapable of resisting him. He didn't love her, and she had no expectations that he ever would now he'd stated that love was an overrated emotion, but he desired her. Perhaps he was right. Perhaps passion and their mutual love for Kazim *was* as good a basis as any for a successful marriage?

'I think the best way for me to adjust to married life is to practise every aspect of it,' she whispered, shocked by her own daring and yet driven by a primitive yearning she barely understood.

With fingers that shook slightly she slid the straps of her chemise down her arms and heard his harsh intake of breath when she peeled the grey silk down over her breasts, her stomach, and finally her hips, and allowed it to pool around her ankles.

She could hear the whisper of a breeze stir the leaves of the palm trees, and the song of some exotic bird, but the silence from Zahir stretched her nerves and she wondered for one terrible moment if she had got it wrong—if he had been turned off by her inexperience or had tired of her already. His slow, sensual smile reassured her, and the molten heat that gleamed from beneath his heavy lids promised heaven.

'Come and swim with me, then, *kalila*,' he invited, and before she realised his intention he'd caught hold of her hand and pulled her into the pool, his mouth capturing her startled cry as they sank beneath the surface.

The water was cool on her heated skin, but Zahir's body was warm when he crushed her against his chest and tangled his legs with hers, holding her so tightly to him that their bodies seemed to be melded together. Erin was out of her depth, and clung to his shoulders. She had closed her eyes when he'd pulled her under, and, deprived of vision, her other senses seemed more acute.

She loved the sensation of his lips moving deliciously on hers beneath the water, of his hands roaming up and down her body before sliding beneath her to cup her bottom. But finally the need for oxygen forced him to propel them upwards, and when they burst through the surface of the pool he broke the kiss, smoothing her tangled curls back from her face.

'Are you sure this is what you want, Aphrodite?'

Zahir's deep, velvet-soft voice resonated through her, and Erin's eyes flew open as she felt his powerful erection nudge between her thighs. Was he going to make love to her in the pool? Excitement cascaded through her, and she nodded wordlessly and wrapped her legs around him in mute invitation.

His husky laughter tickled her ear. 'Patience, *kalila*. This time we will take it slowly, and I will take great care not to hurt you,' he promised as he strode out of the pool and across the sand towards the tent. The friction of her breasts rubbing against his hair-roughened chest caused her nipples to swell and tighten, and she could not restrain a little shiver of pleasurable anticipation at the thought that he would soon be caressing her with his hands and his mouth.

The interior of the tent was cool and dim after the bright light outside. Their bodies were already almost dry from the heat of the sun, but when Zahir set her down he wrapped her in a towel and continued the process with an efficiency that left her tingling all over.

He was not the only one who could tease. 'My turn,' she murmured, taking the towel from him and patting the droplets of water that still clung to his chest hair. She moved the towel lower, totally absorbed in her task, and heard his breath hiss between his teeth when curiosity overcame her shyness and she stroked her fingers along the solid length of his throbbing arousal. Steel wrapped in velvet, she thought wonderingly, surprised by her own daring as she circled him and felt him harden still further in her hands. He was beautiful, like some magnificent sculpture, but instead of being formed from cold marble his skin was warm and satin-soft beneath her fingertips.

Zahir uttered a harsh groan and gripped her wrist. 'Enough, *kalila*,' he muttered hoarsely. Her innocence was indisputable, but she was obviously a born seductress. 'Much more of that and we won't even make it onto the bed. Now it is my turn to prepare you. Lie down,' he commanded softly, his eyes meshing with hers when she complied and stretched out on the silk sheets.

For a moment he simply stood there, staring down at her,

and Erin's breath caught when she saw the gleam of primitive hunger in his gaze.

'You are so beautiful,' he said rawly. 'The moment I saw you I could not take my eyes off you. All I could think of was how quickly I could persuade you into my bed. Now you are my wife, and I find that I am *very* possessive.' He gave a self-derisive laugh and said beneath his breath, 'Which is not something I had expected.'

For a second an emotion crossed his face that Erin could not decipher, but then it was gone, and his slow, sexy smile sent fire thundering through her veins. He came down beside her on the bed and leaned over her to claim her mouth in an unhurried kiss, tracing the shape of her lips with his tongue before dipping between them to initiate a sensual exploration that left her breathless. Then he moved lower, trailing a line of kisses down her throat while he cupped her breasts in his palms and watched her nipples swell as he rolled them gently between finger and thumb.

The feel of his mouth closing around one jutting peak and then the other was so exquisite that Erin whimpered and dug her fingers into his shoulders. She was ready for him, had been since he had stripped by the pool, but he ignored her soft cries that she couldn't wait and slipped his hand between her thighs. He parted her and slid one finger and then two into her molten warmth, gently stretching her in readiness for his full possession. He was determined not to rush her, as he had done the previous night, but the silken evidence that she was fully aroused was seriously testing his self-control, and with a muttered oath he positioned himself above her and dropped a hard kiss on her mouth.

Erin twisted her hips restlessly as the first spasms of

pleasure radiated out from deep in her pelvis. Zahir's wickedly skilful fingers were taking her higher and higher, but she wanted more, wanted to feel him deep inside her, and when he settled himself between her legs she bent her knees, her breath catching as he entered her with one careful thrust. He'd said he would take it slowly this time and he hadn't been joking, she realised when he drew back and then cautiously thrust again, with such exquisite care that tears blurred her eyes.

Last night he had sought to dominate her, but now he was treating her with such gentle respect that her heart ached. This was how it must be between two people who loved each other. But Zahir did not love her. He was simply determined to restore his pride and prove he was not at the mercy of his hormones. Nor did she love *him*, she reminded herself. It was just sex—very, very good sex. She doubted any other man could give her such pleasure, and now she would never find out. She had decided to marry him in a moment of panic, fearing that she would lose Kazim if she did not become his wife, but in her eyes marriage was a lifelong commitment that she was determined to honour.

Zahir suddenly stilled his movements, and his jaw clenched when he caught the shimmer of tears in Erin's eyes. 'You should have told me I was hurting you,' he grated harshly, already withdrawing from her, but Erin slid her arms across his back and tried to urge him forward.

'You're not hurting me, I promise,' she assured him frantically. 'Don't stop, Zahir. Please.' As she spoke she lifted her hips and wrapped her legs tightly around him, and after a moment's hesitation he moved again, gentle at first, then harder and faster, bitterly aware that he could not fight his desperate need for sexual release.

He had never been at the mercy of any woman, and he was always, *always* in control. But Erin blew him away. Perhaps it was the knowledge that he was the only man she had ever known, that her innocent, untutored body had found pleasure only with him. He didn't know, and right now he didn't care—because she suddenly gave a sharp cry and tensed beneath him, the intensity of her climax so strong that he could feel her muscles clench around him, each spasm squeezing him harder until the sensation was unbearably exquisite. He paused, dragged air into his lungs, and made one last valiant attempt to exert control over his body. But it was too late, and as he affected one final, powerful thrust he felt himself explode and spill his seed deep inside her.

For several moments after the last shudders of satisfaction had racked his body he remained slumped on top of her, his face buried between her soft breasts as he inhaled the delicate fragrance of her skin. He knew he should move, that he must be too heavy for her slender frame, but for the first time in his life he was in no haste to withdraw and regain his own personal space. He had never known such a feeling of complete contentment—of body and of spirit. The thought triggered warning bells and he rolled onto his back, irritated by his reluctance to break the contact of skin on skin.

He had married her because she was a good mother to Kazim, he reminded himself. A fact he'd recognised even when he'd suspected her motives for marrying Faisal and adopting his child. Blindingly good sex was a bonus—but that was all it was, a white-hot sexual attraction that had raged between them from day one.

Experience told him that it would probably burn itself out, although right now that was hard to imagine, when the mere sight of tousled red curls tumbling over her white shoulders was enough to make his stomach muscles tighten. But what more could he ask from marriage than a devoted mother to the son he now regarded as his own and sexual satisfaction on tap? He should feel highly pleased with himself, he decided as he rolled onto his side and trailed his hand possessively over Erin's body. No doubt the curious empty feeling inside him was because he hadn't eaten for hours.

# CHAPTER EIGHT

ERIN stirred and opened her eyes to find that it was no longer pitch-black inside the tent but a soft, pearly grey in the hour before dawn. There was plenty of time to go back to sleep, and heaven knew she needed to rest after another night of incredible passion with Zahir, but the memory of how he had made love to her last night, their fifth night in the desert, caused the familiar tug of desire low in her stomach.

She'd learned early on that he liked it when she initiated sex. He was a light sleeper, and she had only to dip beneath the sheets and circle her hand around his manhood and he would respond instantly.

But maybe she should let him sleep, she thought, her lids fluttering down once again. Since their arrival at his camp they had slipped into a routine of rising late and going to bed early, and spent the few remaining hours swimming in the pool or strolling a little way into the desert. Zahir had an extensive knowledge of the plants and the surprising numbers of birds and wildlife that flocked to the oasis. And after the sun had turned into a huge orange ball every evening, and sunk below the horizon, he would stand with her in the quiet desert and point out the hundreds of star formations in the inky sky.

After their stormy wedding night they had settled into an uneasy truce which had developed into a tentative friendship. He was an entertaining companion, and she was fascinated to hear tales of his boyhood, growing up at the palace, and of his close relationship with Faisal. He'd explained that Faisal and his three sisters were his half-siblings, children of King Kahlid's first wife, who had died when Faisal was a baby. Two years after the Queen's death the King had married Zahir's mother, Georgina. Erin had detected from his tone that the marriage had not been a happy one, and although Zahir made light of the fact that Georgina had left Qubbah and returned to America when he was eleven, she wondered if his mistrust of women had anything to do with the fact that his mother had abandoned him.

She should have felt heartened by his genuine interest in her own childhood—it was the biggest sign he had given her that he viewed her as more than simply his sex partner—but she carefully avoided giving details of the appalling lack of care she had suffered during her early years, and the sense of utter loneliness she'd felt living at the children's home.

How could Zahir, who had grown up in a large, loving family, understand that her longing to belong *somewhere* had led her to join the gang that had hung around the shopping mall? Her new 'friends' had been the only people who had ever shown any interest in her. Of course now she looked back and saw how they had used kindness to groom her, but back then she had been a vulnerable teenager, desperate to be accepted by the gang and pathetically grateful for their praise when she proved to be an adept shoplifter for them.

Memories of her childhood reminded her of the vast differences between her and Zahir's social standing, and she had become adept at turning the conversation to other topics. But she could not forget her past, and it gnawed at her confidence. Zahir was a prince, and she shuddered to think of his reaction if he ever learned that her mother had been a prostitute and a drug addict.

She fidgeted restlessly beneath the sheets, knowing she would not fall back to sleep now. The only time she forgot her insecurities was when she was in Zahir's arms, swept up in the world of sensual pleasure he created. She reached across the bed, expecting to feel the solid warmth of his chest, but he wasn't there—and when her eyes flew open she found the bed empty. Despite telling herself that there were any number of reasons why he had left her alone, she could not dispel her feeling of unease—a feeling that increased second by second when he did not reappear.

Should she go and look for him? She had flicked back the sheets and was just sliding her arms into her robe when he walked back into the tent. She knew instantly that something was very wrong.

'What is it?' she asked urgently. 'Kazim…?'

Zahir shook his head. 'He's fine, but my father suffered a heart attack two hours ago.' He ignored her shocked cry and continued in a controlled voice. 'Early indications are that it was a mild attack, but he will remain under close observation by his doctors in the hospital wing of the palace.'

He raked his hand through his hair and frowned at her, as if surprised to see her in her nightgown. 'You must get dressed. We have to return to the palace immediately. Until my father is well enough I will take his place as the King of Qubbah.'

Erin didn't know why his words filled her with such foreboding. She'd known that King Kahlid had appointed Zahir as interim ruler, until the true heir to the throne, Kazim, came of age. But only now did she appreciate the enormity of being the supreme ruler of an entire nation. Already Zahir seemed distant—although that was hardly surprising when he must be worried about his father.

She jumped up and firmly banished her fears that they would never recapture the unexpected closeness they'd shared on their honeymoon. She was Zahir's wife and consort, and she had a duty to aid him in the role that had been thrust upon him. 'I can be ready to leave in five minutes,' she said quietly. He nodded and swung round to walk back out of the tent, but she glimpsed the flare of pain in his eyes and sympathy flooded through her.

He had told her once that he thought love was overrated, but his casual dismissal of the emotion clearly did not include his feelings for his father. He loved the King, and she could not bear to think of his heartbreak if the elderly monarch should not recover. These past few days Zahir had shown her that, far from having a heart of stone, he had a side to him that was kind and patient, gentle, even tender at times. But just because her heart ached for him, it didn't mean she cared about him she reassured herself firmly. She had far more sense than to fall in love with him—didn't she?

'Zahir?' He looked drawn, almost grey, and on impulse she flew across the tent and flung her arms around his waist. 'I'm so sorry about your father. I'm sure he'll be all right.' She wished she could wave a magic wand and restore the King to full health, but of course that was impossible. All she could do was offer Zahir her support.

He stared down at her, frowning slightly, and she had a feeling that his mind was focused on the events unfolding at the palace. But then he cupped her chin and tilted her face, his dark eyes meshing with hers. 'You have a ridiculously soft heart, *kalila*. I would like to share your misplaced optimism, but father is eighty years old and I am well aware that he cannot live for ever. Your concern is touching,' he added coolly, 'but I'm afraid I don't have time to take you to bed right now.'

Erin immediately dropped her arms to her sides, blushing furiously because he had clearly mistaken her gesture of sympathy. 'I didn't expect you to. I wasn't suggesting… I was simply trying to show you that I'm here…if you need me.' She bit her lip, and said in a hurt tone, 'How can you think I would expect you to make love to me when you've just received news that your father is seriously ill?'

'I wasn't complaining about your eagerness for sex, merely about your timing,' Zahir drawled.

His eyes narrowed when she paled, and he resisted the urge to pull her into his arms. He wanted to distance himself from her. The past five days he'd spent with her had been more relaxing than he had expected, and he was surprised at how much he had enjoyed her company—both in bed and out of it. But now it was time to return to the real world. He'd felt ill when he'd first learned of his father's heart attack, but mixed with concern had been an unexpected feeling of regret that he would have to curtail the honeymoon.

Irritation swept through him. For reasons he did not understand Erin had got under his skin. It would be good to get back to the routine of palace life. Once he was immersed in affairs of state he was confident he could relegate her to a small corner of his mind.

'As soon as we arrive at the palace it will be necessary for me to meet with my advisors, and I've no doubt our discussions will continue all day,' he informed her. 'Naturally I will also visit my father, and tonight we will host a pre-arranged banquet in honour of a visiting dignitary.'

The thought of the long hours ahead until he could take her to bed settled like a lead weight in his chest, and he lowered his head to claim her mouth in a brief, hard kiss. Her instant response sent a surge of satisfaction through him, but he forced himself to step away from the temptation of her gorgeous silk-clad body. 'We will both have to learn to curb our impatience, *kalila*. My days will be devoted to duty, but I will expect you in my bed every night.'

Was that to be her only role in his life—as his glorified whore? Erin brooded miserably. She'd thought they had become friends this past week, but perhaps he had only spent time with her because he'd had nothing else to do? 'You make it sound as though sex is the only thing between us,' she said quietly.

Zahir had walked over to the tent entrance, but he turned at her words and his brows lifted. 'It *is* the only thing between us,' he replied coolly. 'What else could there possibly be?'

As Zahir had predicted, his team of advisors were waiting for him when they arrived back at the palace. Even on the journey across the desert he'd had his mobile phone clamped to his ear, and Erin had sat silently beside him, lost in her thoughts. The honeymoon was over, and he had made it abundantly clear that he now viewed her role as his wife as a walk-on part—or perhaps a lie-down part would be a better description? she thought bitterly. But what had she expected? She had married him for Kazim and he had married her for sex—and they had each got what they wanted.

At least she had Kazim, she consoled herself later that evening, when she tucked the toddler into bed. She had missed him desperately, and his evident delight that she was back was a comforting balm to her raw emotions. She was Zahir's wife, a member of the Royal Family of Qubbah, and no one could ever take him away from her now.

But as she prepared for the state banquet her insecurities returned and she felt sick with nerves. She had been horrified when first Bisma and then her two maids had addressed her as 'Your Royal Highness', and even though she was wearing a stunning couture gown—a floor-length cream silk sheath with long sleeves and a decorous neckline—she didn't feel in the least 'royal'. She was a fraud, she thought dismally, and even the fabulous and no doubt priceless pearl and diamond necklace that Zahir had given her on their wedding day, which complemented her breathtaking diamond solitaire engagement ring, could not magically transform her into a princess.

It felt as though butterflies were fluttering in her stomach when she walked down the sweeping staircase, and she was so intent on balancing on her three-inch heels that she missed the flare of heat in Zahir's gaze as he waited for her to join him. She glanced up to find him watching her intently, his eyes hooded so that she had no idea of his thoughts. She wished he would smile at her, maybe take her hand with the easy familiarity he had shown her in the desert. But he was stern and unsmiling and utterly gorgeous in his black dinner jacket and white silk shirt.

Tonight he was the urbane and sophisticated head of the royal family, but on their honeymoon she had been blown away by his raw masculinity. And although she was glad to be back with Kazim, part of her wished she was still at the camp with her desert prince. She had decided this morning that she would not allow him to treat her like a favourite from his harem, that she would not be available for sex whenever it suited him. But one look at his handsome face and the sensual curve of his mouth and she knew she was kidding herself. Her pride was non-existent where he was concerned, and she would take whatever he offered in their marriage— even if it was only his expertise between the sheets.

Praying that she did not look as nervous as she felt, she took Zahir's arm so that he could escort her into the banquet. She was unable to restrain a little shiver of excitement when he bent his head and murmured, 'You are so very beautiful, *kalila*, and I fear this is going to be a *very* long evening.'

He was right. The seven-course meal seemed to drag on for ever, and after several hours Erin's jaw ached from smiling politely while she struggled to make conversation with the elite guests from the wealthiest echelons of society in Qubbah and its neighbouring Arab states. Fraught with nerves, she'd developed a headache soon after she had taken her place at the table, and had stared at the vast display of silver cutlery set in front of her in despair.

The evening was pure torture—made worse when she accidentally knocked over her wine glass and watched in horror as the red stain spread over the pristine damask tablecloth. She didn't belong here in this world of gilded opulence, and she was miserably aware that she was attracting curious stares from the other guests while the servants fussed around her and mopped up the mess. Then a glance along the table revealed that she was using the wrong fork, and she flushed and quickly exchanged it for the right one, conscious that she was being scrutinised by one guest in particular.

The woman was sitting a few places down the table, between Zahir and an older man wearing Arab robes. She was stunningly lovely, with rich, mahogany-coloured hair swept back from her face and slanting dark eyes that at this moment were focused on Erin with an expression of utter loathing. Shaken, Erin stared back at her, but the woman turned her head and spoke animatedly to Zahir, laughing with him and shaking her head so that her ornate diamond and ruby earrings sparkled in the light from the chandeliers above.

'Who is the woman standing with Zahir?' she asked his sister Fatima, when dinner was finally over and the guests were mingling in the Blue Room—so named because of the intricate mosaics of lapis lazuli and gold leaf that adorned the walls.

Fatima glanced across the room. 'Oh, that's Jahmela al Nasser, and her father, Sheikh Fahad. The al Nassers are a very highly respected family in Qubbah, and the Sheikh is one of my father's most trusted and influential advisors.'

Fatima sighed and shrugged her plump shoulders. 'Jahmela is beautiful, isn't she? And she's a gifted academic. She has just returned to Qubbah from England, where she was studying at one of the top universities. Zahir would like to offer her a position on the advisory committee,' she confided to Erin, 'but he knows he will have to introduce the idea slowly if he is not to upset some of the older members, who still cling to the belief that women should not work alongside men in any role. My brother has great plans for Qubbah, and Jahmela will be a strong ally in his bid to persuade foreign investors to back those plans.'

'She's obviously clever as well as beautiful,' Erin murmured, her heart sinking when she thought of the handful of pass grades she had scraped in her basic-level school exams. University had been an unrealistic dream, her main consideration having been to earn a living and support herself once she left the care system, and it was only thanks to her foster parents that she had been able to go to college and train as a nanny.

Fatima nodded. 'Of course the al Nassers had hoped—well, expected really—that Zahir would marry Jahmela. I think the fact that he married you may have caused some friction between my father and Sheikh Fahad. But that is all resolved now, and you mustn't worry about it,' she added quickly when she saw Erin's face fall. 'Forgive me, Erin—I hope I haven't upset you. I shouldn't have mentioned it.'

Clearly embarrassed, Fatima determinedly changed the subject to Kazim, and how fast he was growing. But although Erin smiled and made token conversation, her mind was whirling. If Jahmela's family had expected her to marry Zahir, was *she* the woman he had been engaged to years ago—the woman Bisma had said he had loved? But, if so, why had they not married? It didn't make sense, she brooded miserably as she stared at Zahir. He was smiling at Jahmela and clearly enjoying her company. Perhaps they had argued and broken off their engagement. Was he now regretting his lost chance to marry a beautiful, clever Arab girl who would have made him the perfect wife?

From that moment on the party became a blur of faces and stilted conversation with people she had never met before. She was sure they viewed her as an oddity, with her pale skin and vivid hair—and her glaring lack of sophistication. But until his father had recovered Zahir was King, and one of her wifely duties outside of the bedroom was to act as his social hostess.

No one could say she hadn't tried her best, she brooded

wearily as the last guests were driven away and those who were spending the night at the palace were escorted to the guest wing. Jahmela al Nasser and her father were two such guests, and Erin's spirits had sunk even lower when Fatima had revealed that Zahir had invited them to stay on indefinitely, so that Sheikh Fahad could assist with state affairs.

She was not jealous of Jahmela, Erin assured herself as she preceded Zahir up the stairs, her stiletto heels tapping on the marble floor as she hurried along the corridor to his private apartments. It had been a difficult evening, and she was suddenly desperate to escape his brooding presence—but he was close behind her, and when he touched her arm she whirled around and glared at him.

'I know I'm expected to walk several steps behind you, but no one is watching us and I really don't think it's necessary to stick to the rules of protocol when we're alone,' she snapped irritably.

His brows lifted at her tone. 'I haven't noticed that you ever stick to them,' he murmured dryly. 'You are a law unto yourself, *kalila*.' He ushered her into the apartment and shrugged out of his jacket and tie as he strolled into the sitting room. 'Would you like a nightcap, or coffee?'

'Neither, thanks.' She tore her eyes from the formidable width of his chest and the tanned column of his throat, revealed now he had unfastened his top few shirt buttons. 'I've decided to sleep in my dressing room tonight. I've got a headache.'

Zahir's eyes narrowed at her tone, but he shrugged and murmured coolly, 'That is unfortunate, because I have spent an interminably long day, enlivened only by the promise of your delectable body. I'm sure I don't need to remind you that you are my wife, *kalila*, and tonight I require you to share my bed.'

His supreme arrogance acted like a red rag to a bull, and Erin tossed her hair over her shoulders with an impatient gesture and glared at him. 'What is the point in taking me to bed when we both know you'd rather be with someone else? Or were you planning to have sex with me and pretend that I'm *her*?' she accused wildly.

Black eyebrows winged upwards. 'Pretend that you are who, exactly?'

'Jahmela al Nasser. Do you think I didn't notice how you were all over her at the banquet tonight? The way you smiled at her?'

Erin despised herself for the betraying note of jealousy in her voice. All night she had told herself she couldn't care less about his seeming closeness to his exotic Arabian ex. But the idea that he must have once kissed Jahmela, perhaps made love to her, caused acid to burn in her stomach.

'Fatima told me that Jahmela's family expected you to marry her. I don't know why you broke your engagement, but it was clear tonight that you regret whatever happened in the past. Jahmela is clever and beautiful and she comes from your world. She would have made you a far more suitable wife than me,' she finished miserably.

'Undoubtedly that's true.'

Zahir's calm agreement pierced her heart as if he had fired an arrow through her chest, and the wave of desolation that swept over her made a mockery of her conviction that he meant nothing to her.

He glanced at her speculatively. 'Actually, I was never engaged to Jahmela—although it is true her family had hoped we would marry,' he told her bluntly. 'But I chose you to be my wife.'

'Only because you wanted Kazim—you didn't actually want *me*.'

'I think our wedding night proved conclusively how much I want you,' he murmured sardonically. He came to her with surprising speed and the lithe grace of a big cat, his midnight-dark eyes gleaming beneath heavy lids. 'You know damn well that the moment I saw you I desired you more than I have desired any other woman. You are like a fever in my blood, an addiction I can't control, and if you want the honest truth I resent the hold you have over me.'

He gave a harsh laugh at the stunned disbelief in her eyes, and captured her chin between his fingers, forcing her face up to his. 'My only consolation is that you burn with the same fever, *kalila*. This is just an attention-seeking exercise, isn't it?' he accused her contemptuously. 'I warned you I would be busy once we returned to the palace, but you resent the fact that you are not my most important consideration. In case you've forgotten, my father is lying in the hospital wing recovering from a heart attack,' he bit out furiously. 'And you have no comprehension of my responsibilities as ruler of Qubbah.'

He felt as though he had stepped back in time and was a small boy again, listening to his mother accusing his father of selfishly pursuing his own interests and not paying her enough attention. His parents had married after a whirlwind affair, and the cracks in their relationship had appeared early on—caused, he was sure, by his mother's unrealistic expectations of love. But love played no part in his marriage to Erin, and she needed to understand the ground rules.

'My life is bound by my duty to the kingdom of Qubbah and my responsibilities to my brother's son. And make no mistake,' he warned her harshly, 'they take equal precedence in my priorities. But if you want more of my attention, *kalila*, you can have it.'

'Zahir!' Erin gave a cry of alarm as he swept her up and flung her over his shoulder, his hand clamped firmly on her bottom as he strode into the bedroom. Her temper exploded and she beat her fists on his shoulders. 'How dare you? I demand that you put me down…'

Her feet briefly touched the floor and he spun her round, tugged her zip down her spine and removed her dress before she had time to catch her breath. Her bra went the same way before he lifted her again and threw her onto the bed as if she was a rag doll, his eyes glittering with a mixture of anger and sexual hunger that made Erin's stomach dip.

'At night I'm happy to give you all the attention you could possibly want,' he growled, his shoes, trousers and shirt hitting the floor with barely controlled savagery until he stood in his silk boxers. 'This is the only bed you'll ever sleep in.' The boxers joined the rest of his clothes, revealing his powerful, unashamedly aroused body in all its glory. 'But I wouldn't bank on sleeping for many hours yet.'

Erin stared up at him, her breath coming in shallow gasps as she struggled to control the wild excitement that was pounding through her veins. She was conscious that she was wearing nothing but a pair of tiny lace panties and the priceless pearl necklace, but before she could protest Zahir dragged her knickers down her legs and pushed her thighs apart, exposing her to his heated gaze.

'Pearls suit you,' he drawled lazily, lowering himself onto her so that Erin could feel the solid ridge of his erection stab the soft flesh of her stomach. 'Whenever you wear that necklace to state functions in future I will have a vision of you wearing it as you are now—naked and ready for me.'

She wished she could deny his taunt, but his fingers were probing between her legs and he laughed as he slid into her welcoming wetness. Her weakness for him was humiliating, but desire outstripped her pride and she lifted her hips while he explored her with a merciless skill that set her on fire. He took her to the edge, once, twice, creating a whole new set of sensations when he tormented her nipples with his wicked tongue, and only when she was writhing and sobbing his name did he relent, penetrating her with deep, hard thrusts.

Again and again he drove into her, in a pagan rhythm that took her to a place where nothing mattered but Zahir and her desperate need for him to never, *ever* stop this wild dance. They climaxed simultaneously, a violent explosion of uncontrollable passion that drew a sharp cry from her as he kept her hovering on the brink and then thrust one final time, pumping into her while her muscles clenched around him and her entire body shuddered with sexual ecstasy.

And when Zahir's breathing finally became less ragged and he rolled off her, the slumberous heat in his eyes told her that they had only just begun. He had amazing stamina, and his high sex-drive would demand satisfaction several times before he would allow her to sleep. But of course that was why he had married her, Erin acknowledged bleakly as she rolled onto her side away from him, blinking back tears of self-loathing. Sex on tap with his dutiful wife. And in return she'd got Kazim and a life of unimaginable wealth and luxury.

He had never offered her love and she hadn't expected it—so why did she yearn for him to draw her back into his arms and kiss her with tenderness rather than passion?

She could no longer deny that she had fallen in love with him the moment she'd seen him at Ingledean, totally and irrevocably, and she had been fooling herself that he meant nothing to her. But it was ridiculous to wish for the moon, she told herself sternly, swallowing hard so that he would not guess she was crying.

She felt the mattress dip as he shifted closer, and held her breath when he traced his hand over her hip and then up to curve around one breast. She wished she could control her acute awareness of him, and despised herself for not being stronger. But she knew full well that she would not refuse him—and so did he.

# CHAPTER NINE

ZAHIR shifted fractionally in his chair and nodded encouragingly to the group of school children who were performing a dance on the palace lawn. It had been a busy week, with four state functions including today's garden party. But the past six weeks since he had taken his father's place as ruler of the kingdom had been the same—an endless round of receptions and dinners and meetings with government officials and visiting dignitaries.

It was little wonder that Erin had grown increasingly quiet and withdrawn, he brooded grimly. And although she was smiling at the children, he knew that once she was alone with him she would revert to looking bored and unhappy. It was a look he remembered from his boyhood. His mother's expression of utter tedium and her undisguised frustration with the constraints of palace life were etched on his memory—as were her frequent rows with his father.

Not that Erin voiced her dissatisfaction, but her silent resentment when he made love to her every night evoked an irritating feeling of guilt that he had trapped her in a life she hated. Clearly his optimism during the first weeks of their marriage had been premature. His duties meant that he barely saw her each day, but at night she responded to him with an eagerness that left his body satiated with an excess of pleasure. He felt secretly pleased by her decision to learn Arabic, and he congratulated himself for choosing a bride who was happy to devote her days to their adopted son and her nights to pleasing him.

So where had it gone wrong? Why had Erin suddenly started to pretend she was asleep when he came to bed—which admittedly was often past midnight, by the time he'd finished his discussions with members of his advisory committee. These were exciting times for Qubbah—or would be once he'd finalised his plans for new roads, schools and hospitals, and managed to convince his father and other key elders from the government of the benefits of foreign investment. Jahmela al Nasser's advice was proving invaluable—even if she did talk for hours and drag each meeting on well past the time he'd hoped to finish.

He needed Jahmela, but Erin's unreasonable dislike of her meant that he could not speak of his plans. To his surprise he found that he *wanted* to share his dreams for Qubbah with Erin. But the only time they had alone together was in bed, and in the aftermath of sex the silence between them had grown increasingly tense. His desire for her had not lessened since their marriage, but he was sick of their soulless coupling, and for the past few nights had simply left her to her fake sleep and kept to his side of the bed.

Would she stay, or would she abandon her son and go—as his mother had done? He told himself that he didn't give a damn. He would keep Kazim, and he did not foresee any problems replacing Erin in his bed. For the past six weeks he had worked eighteen-hour days and spent every available

moment of free time with his father. But mercifully the King
had made a good recovery—so why did Zahir feel as though
the weight of the world was sitting on his shoulders?

He was suddenly aware that the children had finished
their dance and everyone was waiting for his response. Erin
had turned her head to him, frowning at his inattention, and
he quickly clapped his hands in applause. Once the dancers
had filed out of the marquee, his personal assistant Omran
appeared at his side and informed him that a group of local
potters had brought their best work for his gracious inspection. Stifling a sigh, he led the royal party out into the
blazing sunshine.

The garden party continued all afternoon, and Zahir was not
in the best of moods when he strode back to the palace. He
suddenly realised that he was too far ahead and slowed his
pace, waiting for Erin to catch up with him. He frowned when
he noted how pale she looked beneath her wide-brimmed hat.
She made no attempt to speed up, and the dejected droop of
her shoulders fuelled his impatience.

'I appreciate that an afternoon spent admiring traditional
crafts and customs is not likely to top your list of exciting ac-
tivities, but must you look as though you've swallowed
poison?' he grated, when she glanced at him listlessly.

'I'm tired,' she replied shortly. 'And I smiled so much this
afternoon that my jaw aches.'

'You have my sympathy, *kalila*.' His tone was laced with
sarcasm. 'But as my wife and consort it is your duty to accompany me to such events.'

'I'm fully aware of my duties, and I have never refused to
fulfil them. Not even when you crawl into bed at two in the

morning,' Erin snapped, blushing furiously when Zahir gave a derisive laugh.

'No, you have never failed to lie back and think of… Well, I'm not sure what you think of in bed, but recently I've felt like I'm making love to an automaton.'

'Perhaps if you dragged yourself away from your beautiful advisor and came to bed earlier, you might find me less tired.'

Zahir shrugged his shoulders dismissively. 'You are always tired lately.'

'Well, I'm sorry if my performance between the sheets isn't up to scratch.'

Erin's tone was icy, but Zahir glimpsed the sheen of tears in her eyes and something tugged at his insides. He hadn't meant the words as a jibe—she really did look tired. There were faint bruises beneath her eyes, and her skin and hair seemed to lack their usual lustre. She'd lost weight too; her fitted green silk jacket emphasised her new slenderness, and her fragile air triggered his concern.

'Erin—' He bit back an oath when he stepped closer and she immediately jerked away from him.

'I'm going to sit by the fountains for a while. It's cooler there,' she said flatly.

'Don't you want to give Kazim his bath?'

She shook her head, and he sensed she was struggling for self-control. 'Not tonight. He'd rather have you anyway. You're his number one person at the moment.'

'It's a boy thing.' He hated tears, but hers were getting to him, especially as she was trying so hard to blink them away. 'I hero-worshipped my father at that age too.' He watched her nod and turn away, but as she walked along the path towards the ornamental pools he called her name, and she looked back warily. 'This evening's banquet to celebrate my father's return to health won't finish late. We'll have an early night, and if you are still tired we could just watch a film and relax.' He hesitated, and then added quietly, 'The past few weeks have been difficult for both of us.'

Erin watched him walk up the palace steps, then stumbled along the path into a secluded area of the garden where the sound of water splashing into azure pools usually soothed her emotions. But after the unexpected gentleness of Zahir's last statement nothing could prevent the tears from spilling down her face, and she sat on the wall and wept at the utter hopelessness of loving a man who had made her his wife but who treated her as his mistress.

Eventually she blew her nose and scrubbed her eyes, and told herself it was her own fault that her head was throbbing. Hadn't she learned as a young child that crying never solved anything? She didn't understand why she felt so over-emotional. Yesterday she'd cried when Kazim had told her he loved her, and today she'd cried because Zahir hadn't and never would. She'd walked into her marriage with her eyes wide open, she reminded herself sternly, and Zahir had always been honest about his reasons for marrying her.

Footsteps sounded on the path, and her heart sank when she looked up and saw Jahmela al Nasser walking towards her. Zahir's stunning advisor was the last person she wanted to see right now.

'Erin! What are you doing out here? I thought you would be hosting the garden party with Zahir.' Jahmela's eyes narrowed on the faint streaks of tears on Erin's face. 'Oh, dear—not a lovers' tiff?'

'Of course not,' Erin replied stiffly. 'The party has finished and Zahir is with Kazim.'

'Even so, you look tired. But I suppose that is to be expected while Zahir's temporary fascination with you remains,' Jahmela drawled, staring down at Erin with an expression of haughty disdain.

'Temporary?' Erin felt her temper stir, but forced herself to remain calm.

Jahmela and her father had remained as guests at the palace since Zahir had taken over as ruler of Qubbah, and during the past weeks she hadn't missed an opportunity to make Erin feel ill-educated and inadequate. Her spiteful barbs had always been carefully worded, and her hostility cloaked beneath exquisite politeness, but now the knives were out and Erin mentally braced herself for battle.

'I am Zahir's wife—that makes our relationship rather more than temporary, wouldn't you say?'

The beautiful Arab girl gave Erin a condescending smile. 'Not when you consider that Zahir only married you so he could be a father to Kazim. Under Qubbah law, when a marriage ends custody of any children is automatically awarded to the husband. The King has assured my father that Zahir will soon divorce you, as he has always planned, and then he will be free to marry me, honouring an arrangement made between our two families several years ago.'

Despite the warmth of the early-evening sunshine, Erin shivered. 'You're talking nonsense,' she said firmly, striving to sound confident despite the sudden lurch of her heart. She was perfectly aware of why Zahir had married her, but he had given no hint that he wanted a divorce. 'Zahir told me he was never engaged to you.' She lifted her chin and glared at Jahmela, trying to ignore the sick feeling in the pit of her stomach.

'He wasn't,' Jahmela agreed, looking surprised. 'I was engaged to Faisal—Zahir was engaged to Maryam.'

The world seemed to tilt alarmingly for a few seconds, and Erin actually gripped the edge of the wall for support. *Zahir and Maryam!* It couldn't possibly be true—could it? 'Bisma told me that Zahir was in love with his fiancée,' she said faintly. 'She doesn't know why the marriage didn't take place.'

Jahmela gave a careless shrug. 'Bisma knows. Everyone at the palace knows that Zahir adored Maryam, and that she eloped with his brother on the eve of their wedding. They were to be married first, and Faisal and me a week later. But instead Faisal and Maryam left a note, saying that they were in love, and then fled abroad, leaving me humiliated and my father furious that our family had been so deeply insulted by the royal family. That is why the King promised that Zahir would marry *me*,' Jahmela said coldly. 'But he suggested that we wait for a few years, until Zahir had come to terms with the fact that he had been betrayed by his brother and the woman he loved. My father allowed me to go to England to study, but now I have my degree and it is time for Zahir to honour the promise made six years ago and make me his Princess.'

Erin shook her head. 'If Zahir had really wanted to marry you, surely he would have done so during the last six years?' she said slowly.

'He was about to,' Jahmela said angrily, her face suddenly contorting into a spiteful mask. 'But then he learned that Faisal had died and that Maryam had lost her life shortly after giving birth to their child. From the moment Zahir discovered Kazim's existence he was utterly determined to claim him—

because Kazim is the only link with the woman he adored. Every time he looks at the boy he sees Maryam. He would have done anything to gain custody of her son—including marrying a nonentity like you,' she added scathingly, her eyes settling on Erin's white face.

She laughed unpleasantly, her sharp glance seeming to see inside Erin's head. 'You're in love with him, aren't you? Oh, my dear, I almost feel sorry for you. Even if Zahir was not still in love with a ghost, he would never love *you*. How could he?' she asked, her brows arching in astonishment at the idea. 'He is a prince, and you are… Well…' Her mouth curved into a cruel smile. 'Let's just say that I was curious to find out more about you, and now I know exactly what you are. If the King knew of your family background, I fear he would not approve of you as Royal Consort.'

Erin shoved her trembling hands in her lap as Jahmela's words fell on her like hammer-blows. She felt strangely light-headed, and was scared she was about to faint, but some last vestige of pride brought her head up. 'Even if everything you say is true, and Zahir is planning to divorce me,' she whispered through numb lips, 'why would you want to marry him, knowing that he is still in love with Maryam?'

'I couldn't care less who he's in love with,' Jahmela said coolly. 'Six years ago I was about to marry a prince and become a member of the royal family. I do not fill my head with stupid dreams of love,' she added contemptuously. 'I want a position within the royal court, and the social standing that comes with being a princess. I am already Zahir's most trusted advisor, and very soon I will be his wife.'

The supreme confidence in Jahmela's voice was the final straw, and Erin staggered to her feet and looked wildly around her. She was going to be sick. There was nothing she could do to prevent it. With a gasp she ran to a nearby bush and retched. It was over in moments, leaving her feeling as though her stomach had been ripped out, and she was shaking, her brow beaded with sweat, when she stumbled back onto the path.

Jahmela was frowning in distaste. 'What's the matter with you? Are you ill?'

Erin shook her head. No way was she going to give Jahmela the satisfaction of knowing how shattering her revelations had been. 'It's nothing. I've been feeling nauseous for the last few days.'

'Really?' Jahmela gave her a speculative look. 'And you've developed a sudden dislike of coffee. You practically turned green when it was served at dinner last night.' Her eyes narrowed. 'I do hope you're not pregnant. That could prove most awkward.'

'I'm not,' Erin denied instantly, but as she made a quick mental calculation her heart missed a beat. 'But I can see why you wouldn't like it if I was.' Erin was down, but Jahmela hadn't won the fight yet. 'Zahir would never divorce me if I was carrying his child.'

'No, he wouldn't,' Jahmela agreed. She waited a heartbeat before dropping her bombshell. 'He would wait until after the child was born before he dismissed you from his life. And, as I have already explained, custody of any child you might have would be automatically awarded to him.'

In less than an hour she was expected to attend the lavish dinner organised in honour of King Kahlid's recovery and his return as supreme ruler of Qubbah. And somehow she was going to have to do so without revealing that she was breaking up inside, Erin acknowledged despairingly as she stared in the mirror at her paper-white face and red-rimmed eyes.

When she had first returned to the palace after her explosive confrontation with Jahmela she'd locked herself in her dressing room and recalled in stunned disbelief everything the young Arab woman had told her. Could it be true? Had Zahir always intended to divorce her once he'd gained custody of Kazim and marry his beautiful advisor?

She did not know how long she'd sat there, but eventually her maid had knocked on the door and reminded her that it was time to prepare for the banquet. She should have made the excuse that she was ill—no one who saw her pallor would fail to believe her. But the steely backbone of pride that had seen her through so many traumas in her life refused to bow to Jahmela's spite, and in fighting spirits she had selected a stunning black velvet floor-length gown which clung to her curves like a second skin. She'd left her hair loose, to tumble down her back in a mass of vibrant curls, but it was going to take a miracle and a lot of make-up to disguise the ravages of her utter misery, she conceded bleakly.

She needed to talk to Zahir, to ask him outright if he was planning to exchange his wife for a more sophisticated model, but she dared not contemplate his reply. Jahmela's taunts echoed in her head while she applied taupe eyeshadow to her lids and highlighted her cheekbones with blusher in a desperate attempt to give her face some colour.

She looked different, somehow, she thought as she stared at her reflection. And she felt different—not to mention permanently nauseous. She couldn't be pregnant. Her period was only a couple of days late. It was only when Jahmela had suggested that she might be carrying Zahir's child that she'd given any thought to contraception—or the fact that they hadn't used any.

The idea that she might have conceived Zahir's baby filled her with a mixture of joy and fear. She would love to have a child, a little brother or sister for Kazim, but the blissful daydream lasted mere seconds. She dared not tell Zahir.

On their honeymoon he had revealed a softer side to him, but she'd rarely seen it since. He had ruthlessly tricked her into bringing Kazim to Qubbah, and she knew with dreadful certainty that if he divorced her he would never allow her to keep any child she might have borne him.

She had no opportunity to confront him before the banquet. He arrived with Jahmela a few minutes late, and remained in deep conversation with her while they waited for the servants to seat them at the table.

To Erin's frustration she was ushered to a chair between two Arab dignitaries, while Zahir took his place between Jahmela and the King. Out of respect for King Kahlid she pinned a smile on her face and tried to join in the conversation, but she was out of her depth with politics and eventually lapsed into silence. Jahmela's confident exchange of views and Zahir's obvious respect for his advisor reinforced Erin's belief that he'd realised he had made a mistake in marrying her, and she picked at the food on her plate, unaware of his concerned glances.

Towards the end of the meal the conversation turned to Kazim—always King Kahlid's favourite subject.

'You must be relieved that your grandson has settled so well at the palace, Your Highness,' Jahmela commented. 'His life here must be very different from the life he led in England.' She paused and looked directly at Erin, a look of undisguised triumph in her eyes. 'And of course *your* circumstances have changed enormously too Erin,' she murmured silkily.

Something in her voice caught the attention of everyone sitting at the table, and Erin's heart jerked painfully in her chest. Suddenly she understood. Jahmela was panicking at the possibility she could be pregnant. She feared that if Zahir learned Erin was expecting his child he would change his mind about divorcing her—or at least postpone his plans to replace her until after the child was born. Jahmela had made it clear earlier that she was utterly intent on becoming Zahir's royal bride, and nothing was going to stop her.

'You must have found the contrast between the deprived housing estate where you grew up and a royal palace quite startling. And presumably now that you have married into money you are no longer tempted to steal—or to follow your mother's…' Jahmela paused delicately '…profession.' She glanced coolly at Zahir, seemingly unfazed by the frown forming on his brow. 'Who would have thought that a prince from the Royal Family of Qubbah would marry a common thief and the daughter of a whore?'

The King and Jahmela's father, Sheikh Fahad, both spoke sharply in Arabic, but Erin did not hear them, nor the murmurs from the other guests who had overheard Jahmela's spiteful attack. Her eyes were drawn to Zahir, to his expression that had begun as a puzzled frown and run the gamut of emotions from confusion and shock to anger.

She was conscious of a strange buzzing in her ears as she scraped back her chair and jumped to her feet. Across the sea of curious faces she spied the doors, but as she was about to flee the King's voice stopped her.

'This cannot be true—can it, Zahir?'

Erin answered before Zahir could reply. 'I'm afraid it is true, Your Highness. I'm sure I am not the sort of person you would wish to be your daughter-in-law.'

Her insecurity and self-doubt were deeply ingrained. Jahmela was right. How could she, with her background and poor education, possibly be a good mother to a future King?

'But you know, don't you, that my position as Zahir's wife was only ever temporary? He married me so that he could be a father to the son of the woman he loved six years ago, and now that he has ensured he has custody of Kazim he will marry Jahmela, as was always planned.'

She ignored the King's low murmur and stared at Zahir, who had risen to his feet, his handsome face drawn into a slashing frown. 'I want you to know that I won't fight the divorce, or…' she faltered, her throat clogged with tears '…or seek custody of Kazim. You were right—he's better off living here, with his family, than with someone from the gutter like me.'

The blue sky was dotted with cotton wool clouds, and the warm breeze carried a scent of lavender and old-fashioned roses. There was no place on earth more beautiful than Ingledean on a spring day, Erin mused—except an oasis in the middle of the desert, where palm trees provided shade from the scorching sun and an azure pool glinted beneath a cloudless sky.

She had been home a month—although Ingledean no longer felt like home without Kazim. The image of his huge brown eyes and impish smile caused the familiar agonising pain in her chest, and she bit down hard on her lip, tasted blood, and cursed the tears that slid unchecked down her face. She couldn't cry for ever. Somehow she was going to have to find the strength to move on, pick up the threads of her life, or maybe make a new one, far away from Ingledean and all its memories. But since she had left Qubbah a terrible lassitude had settled on her, and she could not plan anything when the only two people she loved were far away on the other side of the world.

Was Kazim missing her? she wondered as she scrubbed her eyes with the back of her hand and stared down at the stream that gurgled at the bottom of the garden. She couldn't bear to think of him crying for her. But he was surrounded by people who loved him: Zahir and the King, his nanny Bisma, and all the other members of the royal family. And he was young. He would soon forget her. Leaving him had hurt as much as if she had cut her heart out, but she had only ever wanted what was best for him, and while he undoubtedly belonged in Qubbah she did not.

She'd heard Zahir shouting her name as she had raced out of the banqueting hall after Jahmela's denouncement of her, but the anger in his voice had confirmed her belief that their marriage was over and she hadn't looked back. He was fiercely proud, and would have felt humiliated at learning the truth about her in front of the assembled dignitaries at the banquet.

His personal assistant, Omran, had been hovering in the corridor, and had not bothered to disguise his pleasure when she'd told him she wanted to leave the palace immediately.

'I will instruct Prince Zahir's helicopter pilot to fly you to the international airport. You are already booked onto a flight back to the UK,' he had murmured as she'd emerged red-eyed from the nursery, where she had stood over Kazim's sleeping form and whispered brokenly that she would always love him.

'Already booked?' she had queried, taken aback by the

open dislike in Omran's eyes. 'Did you know what Jahmela was going to say tonight?'

'She is my cousin,' Omran had explained coldly. 'Jahmela has been humiliated not once but twice by the King's sons. It is only right that Prince Zahir should divorce you and marry her.'

Presumably Zahir had already set divorce proceedings in motion, Erin brooded miserably as she wandered aimlessly around the garden.

It was almost two weeks since she had returned his cheque. The sight of his handwriting on the envelope had filled her with a wild and totally unrealistic hope that he had written to ask her to come back to Qubbah. But inside had been a cheque made out for the same ridiculous sum that he had offered her when he had first arrived at Ingledean and tried to buy Kazim. In a furious temper that had preceded a night of tears she had ripped up the cheque and stuffed the pieces back in the envelope with a terse note explaining that she had left Kazim at the palace because she believed it was the best place for him to be. She'd finished by telling Zahir that she hated him, that he Jahmela were welcome to each other, and that she hoped she would *never* set eyes on him again.

She had been lying, of course, she acknowledged despairingly as she watched a butterfly settle on the lilac bush. Its brown and orange wings were so beautiful. Kazim would love to see it. She actually turned to call him, and then gave a choked sob. He wasn't here. Zahir wasn't here. The pain inside her was so raw that she dropped onto the garden bench, buried her head in her arms and wept.

'I suppose it isn't *so* bad here. And the purple heather covering the moors is quite beautiful. But if this is where we're going to live I insist that we have a new central heating system installed before the winter.'

Slowly Erin lowered her hands and pushed her tangled curls out of her eyes. Now she had proof that she was losing her mind. She *couldn't* have heard Zahir's voice, and he *couldn't* really be standing beneath the apple tree, looking heart-stoppingly gorgeous in jeans and a cream shirt, with a butter-soft tan leather jacket slung over one shoulder. Her eyes flew to his face and she blinked, but he was still there, a faint smile on his lips, but a curious, haunted expression in his dark eyes and deep grooves on either side of his mouth.

'What…are you doing here?' Her voice didn't seem to be working properly, and emerged as a croaky whisper.

He shrugged laconically and strolled over to the bench, dropped down next to her and stretched his long legs out in front of him. Erin tensed and her heart jerked painfully in her chest. The tantalising musk of his cologne mingled with the warm male heat of his body made her feel dizzy with longing after a month when she had been starved of him, and when she dared to glance at him she was startled by the answering flare of hunger in his eyes. The sexual chemistry between them had always been overpowering, and she was shocked to realise that despite everything it hadn't faded.

'If you're here to offer me another disgusting cheque, you're risking serious injury with a garden spade,' she told him fiercely, glancing towards the heavy metal tool propped up against the bench.

'No, *kalila*,' he assured her, his voice so grave that her eyes flew to his face. 'I am here because you are here—' He broke off, as if he was struggling to find the right words, and Erin suddenly realised that beneath his relaxed air he was tense, and—incredibly for a man whose arrogance was legendary—unsure of himself. 'You are my wife,' he said in a low tone, 'and I have discovered that wherever you are is the only place I want to be.'

The still silence in the garden that followed his astounding statement was broken by the piercingly sweet song of a blackbird. Erin licked her suddenly dry lips, her heart beating so fast she was sure it would explode. 'I don't understand.'

'It's quite simple.' He sounded impatient and stared at her haughtily. But to her amazement streaks of dull colour highlighted his cheekbones, and his eyes veered from hers as if he was afraid to meet her gaze. 'I love you, Erin.'

Her rebuttal was fierce and immediate. 'No, you don't.'

'I should have known you would want to argue about it, *kalila*.' A little of his tension left him and his smile stole her breath.

'You don't love me,' she said again. It was probably some cruel trick, and she had more sense than to be fooled. 'You married me for Kazim. You love Maryam. Jahmela said so.'

'Jahmela said a lot of things, most of them untrue.' Zahir's voice was suddenly harsh.

'But not the things she said about me,' Erin said thickly. 'My mother *was* a prostitute and I assume that my father was one of her clients. I wasn't conceived from an act of love, but in some dark alley with a stranger who paid for sex. My mother sold her body and spent the money she earned on her drug habit.' She stared down at her hands, not wanting to see the disgust in his eyes. 'We come from vastly different worlds, Zahir, and mine wasn't a nice one. When I was fourteen I joined a street gang and was drawn into a life of crime. I was successfully prosecuted for shoplifting, and it was only because it was my first known offence that I wasn't sent to a juvenile detention centre.'

Zahir's reaction was not what she had expected, and his calm, 'Yes, I heard about that,' brought her head up, her eyes widening at the gentle understanding in his. 'You would have been exonerated if you had explained to the court that you stole those things to protect a younger girl who had been threatened with dire retribution from the gang if she refused to join them.'

'How do you know that?' Erin mumbled, stunned that he seemed to know so much about her.

'I had you investigated immediately after I took you to Qubbah,' he replied, ignoring her gasp. 'My private detective reported back a month or so after we married. I'm afraid Jahmela's party piece did not have the effect she was hoping for, and she has been banished from the palace,' he revealed grimly. 'My father was almost as furious with her for upsetting you as I was, and unfortunately the sudden stress affected his heart. His doctors had to be called to give him oxygen. By the time I was able to leave him, you had gone.' His face tightened. 'Omran had made sure of that.'

'He believes you should marry Jahmela,' Erin said quietly. 'And he's right. She is beautiful and educated and has all the attributes necessary for the wife of the next ruler of Qubbah.'

'Attributes like selflessness and compassion, you mean?' Zahir suggested softly. 'Both those qualities are starkly absent in Jahmela. And yet you—who grew up in dire circumstances, alone and unloved—you have them in abundance.'

'You accused me of marrying Faisal and adopting Kazim simply so that I could inherit Ingledean,' Erin whispered, unable to tear her eyes from the velvet softness of his.

'I could not believe that your love for Kazim was genuine when my own mother had not loved me enough to stick around for my childhood,' Zahir admitted harshly. 'But deep down I knew within days of meeting you—certainly by the time we married—that you were not the gold-digger I had first thought. You were feisty and hot-tempered, and you fought me constantly, but everything you did was for Kazim. You married Faisal knowing that within months you would be solely responsible for a young child, but you willingly sacrificed your youth and freedom because you were determined to give him the loving childhood you never had.

'But then I forced you to marry me,' he continued, looking away from her again, as if he could not bring himself to meet her gaze. 'And you went along with it because you would have done anything rather than be separated from Kazim. And I, who had spent hours torturing myself with images of you and my brother, burning up with jealousy over your relationship with him, discovered too late that you were a virgin. I had to accept that all my preconceived ideas about you were wrong. I stole your innocence, *kalila*, and I was so angry with myself for spoiling something that should have been special for you that I was unnecessarily brutal. You don't know how much I have regretted my treatment of you,' he confessed, in a low tone that was so unlike his usual assured self-confidence. 'I'm not surprised you hate me, Erin, and I deserve it—especially after I sent you that last cheque. It was another test, of course,' he explained, dark colour scorching his cheekbones again. 'Even then I was still frantically trying to prove to myself that you were not worthy of my love.'

Almost as if he could not help himself, he reached out and stroked her hair, winding a silky red curl around his fingers. 'I did not want to love you, *kalila* and I fought hard against it. It's true that I cared for Maryam; she was sweet-natured and gentle and I believed she would make me a good wife. When she eloped with Faisal I was bitterly angry. But it was dented pride rather than a broken heart. Because of that stupid pride I refused to be reunited with my brother, and now it is too late. I won't make the same mistake again.'

He moved suddenly, turned to her and gripped her arms, and she glimpsed the desperation in his eyes as he dragged her against his chest. 'I will do whatever it takes to win you back, *kalila*. You are my wife, the love of my life, and I won't let you go.' He pressed his lips to her temple, his warm breath fanning the curls that framed her face, his eyes closing briefly as if he was in pain. 'I have told my father to name his brother Sulim as the interim ruler of Qubbah in the event of his dying before Kazim comes of age.'

Erin stared at him, shocked beyond words. 'But…but why?' she faltered at last. 'I thought that *you* were to rule until Kazim is older? You are the King's only son, and it is your duty.'

Zahir shook his head. 'My first duty is to my wife, and my father agrees. Although even if he did not I would still be here with you. Don't you understand, *kalila*?' he said urgently. 'You are more important to me than Qubbah, my father— everything. You, me and Kazim, we are a family, and the only thing I want is for us to be together. You love it here at Ingledean, and so we will live here, have our children here—' He broke off when her face flushed with betraying colour and waited for her to speak, but Erin suddenly seemed determined not to look at him.

'Kazim…' she whispered. 'You shouldn't have left him. He'll be distraught without either of us at the palace.'

'I didn't leave him,' Zahir said quietly. 'He's here at Ingledean. Alice has taken him to play in the orchard.'

'Kazim's here!' With a cry Erin tore out of Zahir's grasp and flew across the garden, desperate to find her son.

But as she reached the gate his words finally pierced the air of unreality that had settled on her when he had appeared in the garden and she spun round, her heart contracting when she saw him slumped dejectedly on the bench with his head bowed.

'You love me?' she said slowly, still unable to believe she had heard him right. 'You would really give up everything for me?'

'You *are* everything, *kalila*, and without you I have nothing.'

His head was still lowered, and she walked back to him and dropped to her knees so that she could look into his face. To her astonishment she saw that his eyes were wet, the flare of pain in their dark depths so raw that a lump formed in her throat. She brushed her fingers shakily over his lashes. 'You love me,' she whispered, wonderment flooding through her.

'More than life,' he confessed, his voice thick with emotion. 'Your devotion to Kazim is one of the reasons I adore you, *kalila*, but I am ashamed to say that sometimes I am jealous that he has a place in your heart and I do not. I suppose you think that's pathetic, huh? To be jealous of a three-year-old?' he said heavily.

Erin ran her fingers over his cheekbones, traced his square jaw and brushed a feather-light caress across his lips. 'You don't need to be jealous of Kazim,' she told him gently, feeling a little bubble of happiness form inside her. 'My heart is big enough for both of you. But you, Zahir, *you* are the love of my life, the other half to my soul. The first time I saw you here at Ingledean I knew you were the person I had been waiting for all my life—the only man I will ever love.'

For a few seconds he simply stared at her, a nerve jumping in his cheek. But then, with a groan that seemed to come from the depths of his soul, he lifted her onto his knees, his hands tangling in her hair as he claimed her mouth in a kiss that told her more clearly than words that he would love her for eternity.

'*Kalila*, I missed you so much this past month that I *hurt*,' he growled when he finally released her mouth. He trailed his lips down her throat, his fingers fumbling to unfasten her blouse and then push the material aside so that he could press hot, urgent kisses over the creamy swell of her breasts.

He dispensed with her bra and somehow, without Erin realising how they had got there, they were lying on the grass, and Zahir was kissing her hungrily while he tugged her skirt over her hips. 'Perhaps our first child will be conceived here at Ingledean,' he said huskily, making no apology for his desperate need to make love to her as he tugged at the zip of his jeans and stroked a gentle probing hand between her thighs.

'He or she will be born in Qubbah, which will be our home, where our child's father and brother will one day rule,' Erin stated firmly, her smile taking his breath away as she welcomed him into her. 'We'll bring our child here to Ingledean for holidays. But as for him or her being conceived here—' She broke off as he thrust into her, building her pleasure to a crescendo. 'I'm afraid it's too late for that. I am already expecting your baby. A true child of the desert.'

'*Habibti…*' Zahir's voice shook with emotion as he claimed her mouth in a kiss of tender passion and vowed to love her, Kazim, and all the children he prayed they would one day have, for the rest of their lives and beyond.

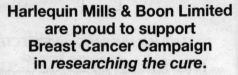

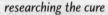

breast
cancer
CAMPAIGN

*researching the cure*

# The facts you need to know:

- Breast cancer is the most common form of cancer in the United Kingdom. **One woman in nine** will be affected by the disease in her lifetime.

- Every year over **44,000** women, **300** men are diagnosed with breast cancer and around **12,500** women and approximately **100** men will die from the disease.

- 80% of all breast cancers occur in post-menopausal women and approximately 8,800 pre-menopausal women are diagnosed with the disease each year.

- However, the five year survival rate has significantly improved, on average today 80% of women diagnosed with the disease will still be alive five years later, compared to 52% thirty years ago.

**Breast Cancer Campaign's mission is to beat breast cancer by funding innovative world-class research to understand how breast cancer develops, leading to improved diagnosis, treatment, prevention and cure.**

# 4 FREE

## BOOKS AND A SURPRISE GIFT!

We would like to take this opportunity to thank you for reading this Mills & Boon® book by offering you the chance to take FOUR more specially selected titles from the Modern™ series absolutely FREE! We're also making this offer to introduce you to the benefits of the Mills & Boon® Book Club—

- ★ **FREE home delivery**
- ★ **FREE gifts and competitions**
- ★ **FREE monthly Newsletter**
- ★ **Exclusive Mills & Boon® Book Club offers**
- ★ **Books available before they're in the shops**

Accepting these FREE books and gift places you under no obligation to buy, you may cancel at any time, even after receiving your free shipment. Simply complete your details below and return the entire page to the address below. You don't even need a stamp!

**YES!** Please send me 4 free Modern books and a surprise gift. I understand that unless you hear from me, I will receive 6 superb new titles every month for just £2.99 each, postage and packing free. I am under no obligation to purchase any books and may cancel my subscription at any time. The free books and gift will be mine to keep in any case.

P8ZED

Ms/Mrs/Miss/Mr ............................................Initials ................................
BLOCK CAPITALS PLEASE

Surname ................................................................................................

Address ................................................................................................

................................................................................................

................................................................Postcode................................

### Send this whole page to:
**UK: FREEPOST CN81, Croydon, CR9 3WZ**